Crudes Castle.

BY MIKE HALE

For our struggle is not against flesh and blood, but against the rulers, against the authorities, against the powers of this dark world and against the spiritual forces of evil in the heavenly realms.

Ephesians. Chapter 6 Verse 12.

Chapter 1. Dream home.

It's a bright morning and the Thomson family have today moved in to a new house in the country, the house is a 17th century house in a village in north England, the village is called Crudes Castle, its home to about sixty people and the village is quite isolated, it is twenty miles away from the nearest town although the village does have a paper shop, a petrol station, a small pub called the Red Dragon and mini supermarket that is usually used by people driving through the village as well as the locals. The Thomson family consists of Danny Thomson, the father he is a successful businessman, with a chain of food factories, it was always his dream to move to the countryside. Sally Thomson is his wife of twenty years, she looks after the children and the house, and she is also very excited about the move. Justin Thomson is eighteen and he is already thinking about moving back to Birmingham, he is "considering his options". Seventeen year old Clare is also considering her options she is also studying business and economics at Collage and hoping to get in to a good university. Fourteen year old Jason is excited about the move but he worries "about starting a new school and making new friends" and seven year old Mandy, Mandy is also nervous about starting a new school. They arrive at their new home 13 Crudes place. Sally notices a brand new car on the drive.

Upon arriving Justin and Clare are amazed and shocked by the size of the house, "it looks fucking creepy" Clare sneers as she gets her first glance at the house, "watch your language" her mom shouts at her, Clare rolls her eyes and look at the house "this place has to be haunted or something" she moans. The Thomson's get out of the car, Dan walks over to the new car parked on the drive "I got this for you" he tells Sally, she runs up to him and gives him a huge hug, "thank you so much" she whispers, Dan smiles, "well I thought you are going to need a car living in the country" he says "come and look inside the house, you're going to love the house" Dan adds, he holds Mandy's hand and starts walking over to the house when he is approached by someone that works for the removal company, "we are done here" he says, "sign here and here" Danny signs by now everyone else is in the house. "Wow" gasps Justin in amazement, "how did you afford this?" Danny laughs, even Clare is pretty impressed, and "wait until you see the bedrooms" Danny excitedly says.

Dan shows them the huge kitchen "no excuse for not being able to cook in nice meal in this kitchen" he jokes, Sally does not look impressed with Dan's sense of humour, Dan guides them in to the living room and shows off the brand new 40 inch television and the leather three piece suite, "I have even got my own little office" he brags, they start walking up the stairs, looking around at some of the old artwork, the house is old and the floor boards are very creaky, Danny leads the way to the bedrooms, Justin and Clare instantly love their bedrooms, they are already starting to see why their dad wanted this place so much. "I bought this place two years ago, I have spent a fortune on the renovation, but look at it now" Danny proudly tells his family, "we are the first people to live in this house for nearly one hundred years" his family continue to look around at their new home, "who were the last people to live here" Justin asks, Danny shrugs his shoulders, "I don't know" he replies, Justin looks at the artwork, he notices some of the art is very dark, "who did you buy it from?" Justin asks, "a very old, very rich couple from London, apparently they were left it in a will over sixty years ago, they never had the time to do anything with it, both of them have had health problems this year and they were pretty desperate to sell, which is why I got it at such a good price" Danny explains with a huge smile on his face.

Clare, Mandy and Sally go down stairs to prepare some food and unpack a few boxes, they do not have much to unpack as Dan had got most of the house ready for his family before they arrived, Dan, Justin and Jason stay upstairs looking at the view of the huge garden, there are hundreds of trees, rose bushes, and in the distance the remains of an ancient castle and village, Crudes Castle "look how big that tree is" Jason says, Justin and Danny look over at the huge oak tree Jason is pointing at "I am no expert on trees but that one must be hundreds of years old" Dan guesses, "this is the life, I am going to hate going back to the city" he adds, his wife shouts to tell them that their food is ready.

Later that night Sally is in Mandy's bedroom trying to get Mandy to sleep, "I want to go home" Mandy whispers "I do not like it here" she adds, Sally tries to comfort her daughter "this is your home now, it's your first night here, just go to sleep and you will feel better in the morning" she explains, Mandy closes her eyes, "goodnight sweetheart, I love you" she whispers and kisses her head before sneaking out of the room, she walks to Jason's door, "you got one hour" she shouts, Jason is busy playing his computer games, "ok" he shouts back. Justin is watching T.V and Clare is revising, Sally and Dan go downstairs and open a bottle of champagne, "lets toast to a happy home" Dan suggest "to a happy home" Sally repeats, they tap glasses, after a few drinks they go to bed, it's now midnight and everyone in the house is sleeping.

Chapter 2. Mrs Morgan.

At 3.00am exactly, Sally is awoken by a loud bang downstairs, "what was that noise?" she gasps as she is shaking her husband to wake him, "what noise, there is no noise" he replies, he turns over and shuts his eyes, suddenly he hears something moving about downstairs "did you hear that" his wife asks, Dan jumps out of his bed, "yes, I did" he replies, he grabs the first thing that he comes across, which happens to be a stainless steel candle holder, the house is very quite they could hear nothing until they hear a painful moan, the moan gets louder and louder, Mandy comes running into her parents' bedroom, closely followed by Clare and Jason.

Danny begins walking down the stairs, he tries to be as quite as he can but every floor board is creaking being quite in a house as old as this house is not easy, he can still hear movement and moaning noises, he is now ready to sneak into the kitchen, although the kitchen is empty Dan senses an atmosphere, as if someone has just left the room. He opens the door to the living room when he sees a figure walking very slowly towards him, it's a very old, very fragile lady she is extremely pale with white hair and bloodshot red eyes, she looks desperate and in pain. Dan notices she has no shoes on and her feet, she is wearing pyjamas and her feet are covered in blood and mud, she holds on to Dan, "you should not be here" she cries, she seems to be struggling to breathe "it is not safe for you, it is not safe for anyone" she collapses, Dan catches her and stops her from falling face first on the floor, "phone a ambulance" he shouts to his wife, his wife runs downstairs and sees the elderly woman unconscious on the sofa. Dan grabs the phone and calls the emergency services.

About twenty minutes later an ambulance arrives closely followed by the police, the police ask every family member what they saw, Detective Mark Green is in charge of questioning, everyone tells what they know, other than Justin, much to his own despair and disappointment Justin slept through the whole incident. The elderly ill looking lady is taken to the local hospital, "where did she come from?" Dan asks the police officers "Its Mrs Morgan, she lives around the corner" Detective Mark Green answers, "she has lived in this village her whole life and she is 107 years old" he adds, Detective Mark Green walks towards the front door Dan thanks the police for coming out and opens the door for them. When the police leave he looks at his wife smiles and says "well that was fucking scary!" they both laugh with a kind of disbelief of what just happened and they go back to bed.

The next day the Thomson's are just about to eat their breakfast when they get a knock at the door, Sally goes to answer it, it's a middle aged couple "hello" Sally says cautiously and nervously, "hello" the man replies "my name is Thomas Morgan and this is my wife Shelly Morgan" he adds, Sally opens the door a touch more, "we have come round to apologize for my gran" he adds "Don't apologize" Sally interrupts, "I just hope she is Ok, have you heard anything from the hospital yet, have you heard how she is doing?" Thomas looks at Sally and says "she is not well before she came out, in fact before coming here she had not stepped foot out of the house for four years, we are surprised she managed to get here" Sally invites them in for a cup of tea, she introduces them to her husband. After introducing themselves and commenting on the "great job" they have done with the house Thomas begins talk about Mrs Morgan, "her name is Victoria, she claims to know things about this village that would make your hairs stand up, she claims that the village was cursed, she claims that her father and a group of locals contained the curse in the year 1920 but she fears that one day the spirits will break free and Crudes Castle will again be cursed" Dan and Sally listen with interest, "of course, it's all a load of bullshit" he adds as he sips his tea, he laughs and Dan and Sally laugh along with him.

Shelly Morgan is not laughing and in a serious tone she adds, "Her husband died twenty five years ago and since that day many people think she has lost her mind, but her father James Green was a powerful, he had connections to the royal family and the government, he was well respected in Crudes Castle, on the 21st December 1920 he and three other locals died trying to contain this curse, nobody knows how they done it but according to Victoria they done it, they contained the curse, Victoria missed her father so much, she was only thirteen" Dan and Sally are again listening intensely, "who cursed the village?" Dan asks, Shelly seems keen to answer but she is interrupted by her husband Thomas "come on dear, we can't stay here talking all day, we got a busy day" he insists, he finishes his cup of tea and walks to the door, "nice meeting you" he says as he shakes Dan's hand "you to" Dan answers, the Morgan's walk out.

As Shelly and Dan walk into the house the phone begins to ring, "Hello" Dan answers and Shelly walks into the kitchen, after two minutes on the phone Dan walks in to the kitchen, his wife looks angry, "don't tell me, you have to go back to Birmingham for a few days?" she guesses, "unfortunately I do" Dan answers "but this will be the last time for a few weeks" he promises, "after what happened last night, I am scared to be here alone" Sally replies, but she knows that Dan has no choice he must go back, "make sure you lock all the doors and windows and you will be alright" Dan says as he goes upstairs to pack some clothes, "I will start out in the morning so you will only have two nights alone" he adds, "they were locked last night" Sally insists, Dan walks back down the stairs, "they could not have been locked or she would not have been able to enter the house" he points out but Sally is sure that she locked the doors and windows.

Chapter 3. Cockroaches.

Its 9.00pm and Dan has to be up early in the morning so he decides to go to bed, he goes in to Mandy's bedroom and says goodnight, he explains that he will not be there for a couple of nights, Mandy gives her dad a kiss and closes her eyes. He enters Jason's room but Jason is too busy playing his computer to pay attention to anything that his dad says, Dan says goodnight and walks in to his own bedroom. Meanwhile Justin and Mandy are watching television downstairs, until they are interrupted by a loud scream coming from the kitchen, Justin and Mandy both run in to the kitchen, only to see Sally backed up in to the corner of the room pointing at the floor, they both look to where she is pointing, "it's just a fuckin cockroach" Justin says, Dan comes running in to the kitchen, "what is going on?" he asks, "there is a cockroach in the kitchen" Justin answers with a hint of sarcasm, Dan looks at the cockroach and stamps on "I thought it was something serious" he moans, "I have a long day tomorrow, I would like to get some sleep" he adds "it is serious" Sally insists, "they are disgusting and I do not want them in my house" Dan rolls his eyes "we live in the countryside now, you're going to get insects in the country" he calmly explains, "not in this house" Sally answers. Dan walks back up the stairs, shaking his head.

It's 5.00am and Dan's alarm clock is bleeping, he gets out of bed and brushes his teeth and has a shower, after twenty minutes he walks in to the bedroom sits on the bed and kisses Sally's head "I am goin to work now" he whispers "goodbye, love you" she says and Dan heads off to work. Sally gets up at 8.00am, she wakes Mandy, Jason, Justin and Clare and heads in to the kitchen to do them some breakfast, when she enters the kitchen she is horrified to see three more cockroaches, she picks up a newspaper, rolls it up and squashes the cockroaches with it, as she is cleaning up the mess something catches her eye, she notices a huge beetle walking across the kitchen, she squashes it, Sally is truly disgusted by the bugs.

Sally puts the T.V on and starts tidying the living room, when suddenly she starts to get a strange feeling that she is being watched, she stops what she is doing and starts to look around the room, she does not know what she is looking for but the feeling will not go away, in fact the feeling is getting stronger and Sally feels scared, she looks at the television to see a choir singing songs of praise, but she notices one member of the choir is not singing, they are standing still looking at the camera, the camera angle changes and it makes it hard for Sally to focus, until she gets a more clear look at her, she sees the long white hair and the pale skin, "mom" she hears, she jumps in fright "don't do that Justin" she shouts, Justin laughs uncontrollably, Sally shakes her head, she looks at the television but the woman she thought she could see was gone, "We are going to the castle today" Justin tells his mom, "what for?" she asks, "to look around it" Justin answers, "there is not many tourist attractions round here" Clare adds.

Chapter 4. Crudes Castle.

Justin and Clare are at Crudes castle, around the castle are the ruins of an ancient village, not far away they see a circle of nine standing stones, Justin is very fascinated by the castle, the village and the stones "the stones must date back thousands of years and castle hundreds of years" he explains to Clare, Clare is too busy drawing and not really listening to Justin, Justin walks in to the castle. he looks around, he notices the walls look black, as if there was a fire, suddenly he hears movement, he begins to listen for a noise but the sound has gone, he starts walks towards the door when he sees a masked man running towards him, he screams in absolute panic and runs outside the castle, when he gets out of the castle he falls in a puddle of mud when he is lying in the puddle he hears laughing, he turns around to see what is going on, the man removes his mask, "I am just having a laugh he shouts my name is John Jackson, and I am sorry for scaring you like that" Clare laughs Justin does not.

Two teenagers approach John, "this his Jack Gould and Anthony Collins " John announces, Jack and Ant are still laughing and mocking Justin, "the fuckin pussy shit himself" Jack giggles, Justin feels embarrassed and angry at the same time he tries to wipe the mud from him but he is covered, he wants to say something but he is scared after all John looks like he is in his twenties and he is outnumbered. To make Justin even more angry he notices that John is taking a keen interest in his sister and she does not seem to mind, "come on Clare its nearly three O clock we should go home" he says, John looks at Clare "don't go" he pleads, Clare smiles, Ant and Jack are still laughing at Justin whom is becoming more annoyed by the minute, "I should go" Clare insists, "we got alcohol" John brags, he walks up to Ant and snatches a carrier bag from him, with a huge grin on his face he pulls out a bottle of Vodka and a bottle of Jack Daniels, "we also have plastic cups and weed" he brags, Clare looks at Justin "one drink?" she asks, "whatever" Justin replies.

"Come on" John says excitedly as he starts walking to the castle, Ant and Jack follow, Clare quickly packs her art and puts it in to a folder and follows them, Justin does not really want to be there, he is scared of John and the other two are still laughing at him and making him feel uncomfortable, but he knows he cannot leave his sister with them so the reluctantly follows. John gets some plastic cups out of the bag and pours everyone a generous shot, Justin hears Ant and Jack whispering about him and laughing, "what the fuck are you laughing at?" he aggressively asks, they stop laughing, "you" Jack answers, Justin rushes towards him and throws a punch which hits Jack in the face, John quickly steps in the middle of the "calm down ladies" he jokes, Justin is still angry but Jack has blood coming from his nose, he smiles, "yo, I'm sorry" he says as he walks towards him to shake Justin's hand, Justin rejects the handshake and turns the other way.

John pulls a bag of weed starts rolling a spliff, Justin has never tried drugs and he is not a drinker, despite this he downs his vodka John pours him another one, Justin thinks that he can hear Jack and Ant laughing at him as he downs his second vodka, Clare is more cautious but Justin is trying to prove a point so covered in mud he necks his third shot. Ten minutes later and Justin is now feeling weird, he feels drunk but also relaxed, he seems to be losing control of his legs, Justin looks at Jack and Ant they both start historically laughing at him, Justin is not feeling angry, he feels paranoid and scared, he looks at John and sees Clare in his arms, "what are you doing?" he asks, Clare and John look at Justin and laugh, by now everyone there is laughing at Justin, he feels light headed, confused and he does not know what is going on, Justin runs out to the back of the castle.

He steps outside and notices a strange low cloud coming towards him, suddenly a strange, dense mist surrounds him and the castle, meanwhile inside the castle Clare demands they look for Justin, "we will never find him with this mist" Jack points out, but Clare does not take no for an answer, they decide to separate, John and Clare go around the back, the other two around the front "make sure your back here in twenty minutes" Clare instructs. Justin is now walking in the mist he is lost, scared and confused, when he spots a group of people in the distance, he walks towards them as fast as he can, the mist is making it hard to see but as Justin gets closer he notices the group are wearing black hooded robes and chanting strange repetitive chants, they are looking right at him and they look angry. Justin hears a baby crying, he looks around and sees a baby lying on a small stone in the centre of the stones, he sees that a child sacrifice is taking place and shouts at the top of his voice "murderers, help, murderers" by now all the hooded men are quickly walking towards him, Justin begins to run as fast as he can.

He runs the opposite way back towards the back of the castle, when he enters the castle he sees that the mist has gone so he runs to the front entrance and steps outside the castle, when he looks up he sees people everywhere, the ancient village seems to be alive and Justin does not want to be there, he notices that the castle has guards armed with huge swords. Justin runs out of the castle and in to the village, the sewage waste flows through the street and the people look rough, weak and ill, he feels the locals staring at him and he begins to feel very uncomfortable and then he notices something, the people seem afraid, there is panic all around him, "what is happening" Justin thinks out loud, they're coming a terrified local tells him, "who" Justin asked but the man fled before answering.

Justin sees something in the distance, but he cannot make out what it is, he looks around and notices the trees have no leaves on them, he notices all the children look ill as do their parents, the village is run down. It's as if the people are ageing by the minute, dead bodies lay all over the village, Justin sees two strange dark figures in the distance, he notices that these figures are not panicking, he tries to have a good look but he cannot see their faces, the figures are watching the desperate villagers and their children, Justin looks around and sees even the trees are dying as is the grass. The figures are coming closer they seem to be enjoying the chaos, as they get closer Justin gets eye contact with one of the strange dark figures, the sight of the figures face horrifies Justin, he hairs stand up and his body temporarily freezes as he sees the creature is looking straight at him, Justin feels someone breathing on his neck, he turns around to see a old lady with long white hair looking back at him, he sees the creatures quickly approaching "wake up" she shouts, Justin wakes on the floor of the dark castle, he looks up and sees John, Jack and Ant and then he sees Clare "come on lets go home" Clare says, they start walking home.

Chapter 5. Still trippin.

By now its 10.00pm Clare and Justin walk in to the house, "mum" Clare shouts "mum, where are you?" she shouts again, "I'm in the kitchen" she hears her mother answer, Justin is holding on to Clare to prevent him from falling flat on his face, as Clare and Justin walk in to the kitchen they discover their mother on her hands and knees, "what are you doing?" Clare asks, "they are coming from under here" Sally replies, "mom" Clare says "but I cannot reach them, I am going to have to move these units" Sally adds, "mom" Clare repeats, "we might need pest control" "mum" Clare screams at the top of her voice, Sally finally looks at them, she notices that Justin does not look right as his sister holds on to him. She stands up quickly "oh my God" she gasps, "are you alright son?" she asks, Justin looks spaced and he is still covered in mud, "what the fuck has happened to him?" Sally asks Clare begins to cry.

Clare tells how they meet three men at the castle, she tells her mom of the pranks they were playing on Justin and how Justin was starting to become angry and he wanted to leave. Clare starts hysterically crying, Sally has little sympathy "what happened?" she asks sternly, Clare stops crying regains her composure "they poured him a drink of vodka, he drank it, then he had another and another, then he started acting really strange" Sally looks over at Justin, he is sitting on the floor laughing to himself, "at first I thought he was drunk but then he started screaming, screaming with real fear, he scared me, then he then run off, we lost him" Clare pours herself drink of water and takes a sip "we went looking for him but the mist made it impossible to find him, that's when they told me they had slipped something in his drink" Sally looks fuming "what did they put in his drink?" she asks, Clare starts crying again "I dunno acid or something" she sobs.

Sally runs over to Justin and looks in to his eyes "his pupils are dilated" she says, she starts to talk to him "how you feeling hun" she asks him "I'm tired" Justin answers, "you should have some water and go to bed, I will do your water" Sally insists, Justin starts walking up the stairs, Sally walks in the kitchen to do him a drink when she notice cockroaches on the floor and she starts killing them, a couple run under the fridge, she pours Justin a drink and walks upstairs. She looks in to Mandy's room she is sleeping, Jason is busy playing his computer again, she takes the drink in to Justin, Justin has a sip of water and gets in to bed, it does not take long for him to sleep. Sally goes downstairs and phones her husband, Dan is his hotel in bed watching TV, he answers the phone, "Hello" his wife says, Dan knows by the tone of her voice something is wrong, "what's up?" he asks, Sally explains what happened, "is he alright now?" Dan asks, "he is sleeping"

Sally answers, she begins to cry, "I am coming back in the morning" Dan says, "I would come back now but I need to take care of something in the morning" he says, he promises to be back home by dinner time.

The next day comes and Justin wakes up, it's a bright day and Justin has a painful headache, he remembers the night before the same way we remember dreams, he walks out of his bedroom and to the stairs, he feels ill and slightly dizzy as he walks down the steps, he goes straight to the kitchen "how you feeling" his mom asks, "I feel better but I have a nasty headache" he says as he pours himself a glass of orange juice and walks in to the living room, "your dad is coming back" Sally shouts to him, "he doesn't need to do that, I am fine" he shouts back. Clare is reading a book and Mandy and Jason are watching TV, Clare looks up and smiles at him, Justin smiles back "what the fuck happened?" Justin asks, Clare tells him the whole story, he is angry when the discovers the truth, he sits down and starts staring at the TV, he is not watching TV he is thinking about what happened and what he seen, Justin is traumatized by what happened.

Justin thinks about the hooded men at the standing stones, he then remembers entering the castle, he thinks about the guards carrying massive swords, to Justin everything felt so real, he is thinking hard. Justin has many thoughts running through his head, the hallucinations, John, Jack and Ant laughing at him, the guards and the dark figures watching as the village seemed to dying in front of his eyes, he is lost in his thoughts. Suddenly he stops thinking, he is back in the room sitting on the chair, but the room feels cold and the chair feels damp, he looks at the chair, it looks dirty, old and mouldy and there are insects all over it. He jumps up off the chair "fuck" he shouts, then he starts looking around the room, the whole room looks the same, dirty, worn and old.

He starts running around the house in a huge panic "what the fuck is going on" he screams, he notices pictures are hung on the wall, he picks one wipes the dust off the glass, he is shocked and horrified to see it's a family picture that was taken just before the move, he throws the picture to the other side of the room, the picture frame is heavy it smashes one of the dirty windows. Something outside catches Justin's eye, it looks different, he walks closer to the window to get a better view, standing on cockroaches and insects with nearly every step he takes, when he gets to the window he notices the trees have no leaves but that's not all the grass is brown the whole place looks dull he also notices a strong strange smell, then he sees something in the distance, a dark shadowy figure, the same as he seen at the village when he was under the influence of mind altering, hallucinogenic drugs. A noise in the kitchen distracts him, he picks up the first thing he sees, which is a empty bottle of wine, he begins to sneak in to the kitchen, when he enters the kitchen he notices it's a different lay out, some of the units that were on the back wall have gone and there is a hole in the wall, he walks up to this hole, its pitch black inside, he hears something from the hole, he turns around to get a torch from the drawer when he turns round to look he is confronted by an old lady with long white hair "get out, now" she screams, "do not go down there" she screams out loud, Justin sees her bloodshot eyes, pale skin and yellow teeth he also sees fear and terror in her face, he turns white and falls to the floor.

When he looks up the room looks different "Justin, Justin" he hears, he regains his focus only to see his mother looking down at him "what's wrong?" she asks in a concerned voice, "you broke the window" Clare adds, Justin stands up, his mom tries to help but he shrugs her away, "I am alright" he claims, "what happened?" his mom asks, Justin thinks about it, "It's like I am in a different world, a world of demons and ghosts" he says, "well you're not" Clare points out, "you are in our world, throwing things around the living room, breaking windows and acting like a freak" she adds, Justin sits down, "shut up" he orders, "I have an headache"

It's 11.30am and as promised Dan is back but he is not happy, he walks in to the house, his wife sees him enter the house, "how is Justin?" Dan asks, Clare walks in to the hallway, "he's still trippin!" she tells him, Dan walks in to the living room to see him, Justin is sleeping on the sofa it is obvious to Dan and the rest of the family that Justin is having disturbing dreams he is moving around moaning as he sleeps, he looks pale and is dripping from his forehead. Mandy and Jason are still watching TV, Dan turns around and looks at Clare "I want to know what happened" Clare is forced to tell the story again. After hearing the story Clare's dad is livid, he paces round the room thinking, "get in the car" he drags Clare in to the car, "I am going to find them and you are going to help me find" he orders, Clare agrees, after driving up to Crudes castle, the local shop around, the pub and up and down the street a few times, Dan notices three men coming out of the pub, one of them has a carrier bag, Dan looks at Clare, Clare looks at the men, "that is them" she says, Dan drives past having a good look at them, Clare looks the opposite way, she does not want to be seen "what the fuck you looking at?" John shouts the other two laugh, Dan drives past them, "I am going to get them, you wait and see" he drives back home. When he gets home he goes straight for the phone, Clare worries about what he might be getting up to, "dad isn't going to do anything crazy is he?" she asks her mom, "I don't know" Sally answers.

Justin sleeps until 5.30pm, as he wakes he feels a lot better the headache has eased and he feels more energetic, he walks straight to the fridge and he pours himself a glass of juice he drinks it in one swig, he notices large two cockroaches on the floor and he stamps on them both, Dan and Sally walk in to the house, Dan walks up to his son, "how you doin?" he asked, "I feel loads better" Justin answers, his mom looks right in to his eyes and says, "you look loads better" Justin Smiles.

Chapter 6. Nightmares.

A couple of months has passed since Justin's experience, the hallucinations still haunt him to this day in his dreams when he sleeps and in his mind when he is awake, he still sees the elderly woman when he sleeps, he gets the feeling she is trying to tell him something but fear of her stops him from listening to her. The cockroach problem has got worse, yet they cannot find where the cockroaches are coming from, Sally is phoning pest control companies, "they are coming out next week" Sally tells Dan, "how much is that going to cost?" Dan asks, Sally picks up the leaflet, "they will give us a quote" she answers, Dan is just about to argue his point when he spots a huge cockroach, he puts a glass over it, "that is the ugliest thing I have ever since" he covers the top of the glass and shows his wife and says, "we best let them give us a quote, I think" he takes it outside and stamps on it.

Later that day Mandy and Jason are eating their food, until Sally opens the fridge and discovers six cockroaches in the fridge, she runs to the children, "sorry, you cannot eat this" she insists as she is throwing it in the bin, Jason is annoyed, "I'm starving hungry" he shouts, "I want food, I want food" he starts chanting, Sally rolls her eyes, she picks up the phone and calls Dan, he picks up, she explains about the cockroaches in the fridge, "can you pick some food up for the kids on your way back?" she asks "I will" Dan answers, Dan makes his way to the local garage and mini supermarket to collect some food. When walking around the shop Dan sees a cockroach, "not just our house then" he thinks to himself, he gets the food and starts driving back home. That's when he crosses paths with John, Jack and Ant, he did not like these kids after what they had done to his son, but he had promised his wife that he would not go after them but just looking at them makes his blood boil. They are arrogant, disrespectful bullies he watches them as he drives past, "fuckin pricks" he angrily mutters to himself.

Meanwhile Sally is in the kitchen she is cleaning out the fridge, she hears Mandy talking to somebody, but she does not hear anybody talking back to her, she walks in to the living room, "Mandy, who you talking to?" she asks, Mandy turns around to look at her mother, "Mrs Morgan" Mandy replies before Sally even gets chance to ask anything else Dan walks back in to the house, Sally approaches Dan and explains what Mandy told her, Dan dismisses it as "rubbish" and this annoys Sally, Dan looks at her and explains "Mrs Morgan can hardly walk, I doubt she come in to the house, had a conversation with our seven year old child and the escaped because she heard you coming, it sounds farfetched" Sally sees his point, "but sometimes I get the feeling I am being watched" she argues, Dan laughs "paranoia" he claims, Sally believes he may be right. She changes the subject to the cockroaches, "we have cockroaches everywhere" she claims, "the problem seems to have got worse as the day as gone on, not only that they seem bigger and uglier than normal cockroaches" she adds, Dan insists that she has nothing to worry about, "we have pest control coming out next week, let's just see what they say" Dan calmly requests.

The next day comes, its 7.00am Sally and Dan are woken by the alarm clock, they wake Mandy and Jason for school and Clare for college, when they get down stairs and they are faced with cockroaches everywhere, Dan and Clare kill over forty cockroaches between them. Sally looks at Jason he is falling to sleep while he waits for his breakfast "I told you to go to bed earlier, what time did you finish playing the computer?" she asks, he opens his bloodshot eyes, "I went to bed at ten, like you told me to" he replies, Sally hands him his breakfast, "why are you so tired then" she asks, Jason begins playing his handheld computer, "I was having bad dreams, they were keeping me up all night" he explains, Sally walks up to him and grabs the handheld computer from him, "playing these silly games all night is probably causing your nightmares" she tells him, she puts the handheld computer in her bag, "come on your going to be late for school" she tells Mandy and Jason, Mandy starts eating faster, Jason still looks half asleep, she walks in to Dan's office and tells him "I am not taking Jason to school today, he hardly slept last night" Dan is very busy typing, "it is up to you" Dan answers, and immediately starts typing again, Sally walks out, "wait here" she tells Jason, "I am dropping your sister off, you can take the day off" she adds, Jason sits down in the front room and starts watching TV happy to get the day off.

Its mid day before Justin gets out of bed, Dan is disgraced by this "what time do you call this?" he asks, Justin looks at his watch and sarcastically answers "half past twelve, what time do you call it" Dan is fuming at Jason's laziness, he walks out of the room and in to his office, Sally follows him, "that kid is a waste of space" he tells his wife, Sally tells him to "calm down and lay off Justin" "he needs to man up a bit" his dad insists, Sally walks out of the room, killing a cockroach on the way out. She does Jason some beans on toast, just as she hands him his food her phone starts ringing, she looks at the phone and sees its the school so she answers the phone, "can I speak to the parent of Mandy Thomson please" the school secretary asks, "speaking" Sally replies, "your daughter has been complaining of being tired all day" Sally is told, "she fell to sleep in lesson" the secretary adds, "give me fifteen minutes" Sally replies, she puts the phone down, tells Jason where she is going and rushes to the school to collect Mandy.

After about half an hour Sally gets back from the school, Mandy looks very tired, "what's wrong, sweetheart?" her dad asks, "I am just tired" Mandy answers, "well if you want to chill, you, your mommy and Jason can watch a film if you like?" Jason jumps up off the sofa "can we watch Scarface?" Sally shakes her head "no, we have got to watch something suitable for Mandy" she answers, "boring" Jason moans, Dan goes back to his office, he has been on the phone all day. After half an hour Dan walks out from his office and in to the living room, "would you like a cup of coffee?" he asks Sally, there is no answer, he walks round to see their faces, Sally, Jason and Mandy are fast asleep on the sofa, Dan walks out the room and shuts the door.

Clare has finished college early she is waiting for a bus to take her from town to the village of Crudes Castle, Clare also did not get much sleep last night, although she never does when she is revising and stressed about exams, after a twenty minute wait the bus pulls up, Clare gets on and she looks around the bus, there are only four other passengers on the bus, Sally she walks to the back of the bus, and she sits down, she puts her headphones on and she puts her music up loud. She feels tired her eyes begin to close, before she knows it she is back home, the journey does not seem to take as long as usual to her, the bus stops, Clare steps out, something feels different, she starts walking towards her house. She walks down the garden, when she looks up at the house she notices the house looks different, this leads her to believe she has entered the wrong property, until she sees the address on the post box, 13 Crudes Place, she looks back at the house.

Meanwhile Sally, Mandy and Jason are still sleeping until Sally wakes up, Sally notices the sofa is damp and dirty, she puts her hand on it, it's soaking wet, she looks at what she is sitting on and jumps off screaming, Mandy and Jason wake up, "what's wrong?" Jason asks, then he notices that the house does not look the same as it did, it looks dark, dirty and extremely run down, the sofa is black with dirt and crawling with insects, Jason and Mandy notice huge cockroaches, there are literally hundreds, crawling on the floor and on the furniture, Sally is still looking around in shock, "where are we?" she thinks out loud, suddenly Mandy screams, Sally looks at her and sees that she has a huge Beatle crawling up her, Sally quickly picks her up and knocks it off, stamping on it as they hit the ground, Sally looks up and notices a glowing figure slowly walking towards them, "help" Sally screams, nobody hears, "help" she shouts again, and once again nobody hears her desperate screams.

Clare gets to the front door "what the fuck is going on" she gasps to herself, the door looks old and rotten in places, Clare walks away from the house, she gets a feeling that she is not alone, she looks around at the dying trees and the brown grass and she notices that even the evergreen trees are brown, everything she can see appears to be dying, Clare looks in the distance, she can hear noises, she walks out of the garden and back on to the road, after five minutes of walking about the street she realizes, the whole place looks dull, run down and lifeless, until she hears something again the noises are getting louder, they sound like screaming, Clare still feels she is being watched.

Sally looks straight at the face of the glowing figure in the living room, she recognizes the face, its Mrs Morgan, she looks even more frail then she did the last time Sally seen her, Sally watches Mrs Morgan as Mrs Morgan struggles to walk to the window, she turns around and looks at Sally, "come here" she weakly mutters, Mandy is holding on to her mother's legs, Sally picks Mandy up, she looks at Jason and Jason looks back at his mother, at the same time Jason and Sally make a run for the door in a desperate attempt to escape from the room, the door slams before they manage to get out, "I am not going to hurt you" Mrs Morgan explains, "now come and see" Sally puts Mandy on the floor and she tells Jason to wait where he is. Mrs Morgan points to the window, Sally looks at the window she sees a strange dark figure outside in the distance, then she see's Clare and John, "Clare" she shouts, she looks again and Clare is gone, Sally looks at Mrs Morgan, Mrs Morgan grabs Sally's arm very tightly for an old lady, "get out of this house" Mrs Morgan demands, "before you die" she adds, Sally wakes up, as do Jason and Mandy.

Clare is about to enter the house when she hears movement behind her, she turns around to investigate, its John "what is goin on?" she asks him, John looks at Clare and then seems to look at something behind her, his eyes widen and his face changes to a face of sheer panic and terror, Clare turns around to see what he is looking at, Clare hears her mother calling in the distance, she then see's a group of black hooded figures looking at her and John, she cannot see their faces but she does notice John is terrified by the sight of these men, she looks again this time she gets a glance at one of their faces, it's the most hideous, evil looking face she has ever seen, she screams in sheer terror, then she wakes up screaming on a empty bus "are you alright?" the bus driver asks "I'm fine thank you" Sally answers she is only one stop from home, Clare is horrified by the dream.

Sally tells Dan of her strange dream, she explains that the children were there and they had dreamt it to, "it felt so real" she says. She explains that Clare was there to, "surrounded by strange hooded men" Justin over hears the conversation, "I have seen them to" he interrupts, Sally and Dan both look at him, "when did you see them?" Sally asks, "I seen them when I was hallucinating" he answers, "What is going on?" Sally gasps, Dan rolls his eyes in disbelief, "hello" he shouts, "he was hallucinating! And you was dreaming, it's not real, none of this is real" he shouts, Sally shakes her head, "it feels real to me" she insists. Clare walks in to the house, "what's all the arguing for?" she asks, Sally quickly walks up to Clare "have you seen men wearing hooded cloaks anywhere?" Clare is instantly reminded of her dream, "no" she answers, Dan looks over at Sally when Clare adds, "but I have just had the strangest dream" Dan's head quickly turns to Clare, Clare begins to explain "I was here but the house looked old and run done, the whole place looked old and run down" Justin interrupts, "like the place is dying?" Clare looks at him, "yes" she answers, "I seen it to, I seen you there" Sally tells Clare, "I seen you in my dream, you was with that man that give Justin the drugs" she adds, Clare looks at her mother, "how can that be?" asks Clare, Dan remains sceptical "have you ever thought it could be a coincidence, you could have watched something on TV that stuck in your heads and came out as a dream?" he rationally explains..

Chapter 7. The Ram.

Later that week and the strange disturbing dreams have not reoccurred, the cockroach problem however has worsened, cockroaches are now everywhere, even upstairs, the children have cockroach bites on them, and they are finding dead cockroaches and cockroach excrement all over the house.

Meanwhile Dan is having a busy and stressful day at work worrying about his businesses finances, its lunchtime so he goes in to Birmingham city centre to get some food, the city is busy, Dan notices a familiar face in the crowd, she is looking right at him, he sees her long white hair and he believes it to be Mrs Morgan, but there are too many people in the way, he tries to walk towards her as fast as he can, but more and more are blocking him and getting in his way, he gets past the crowd and sees her watching him, he walks quickly towards her until he collides with a woman knocking her to the floor, "I'm so sorry" he says as he is picking her up, she looks angry but she replies "not to worry" and storms off, Dan quickly looks around him but Mrs Morgan has gone, Dan is then approached by a old homeless woman, "you are surrounded by evil spirits" she tells him "you are in great danger, you are cursed" he looks in to the shop window, where he should see the reflection of an homeless woman but instead he sees the reflection of Mr Morgan, the homeless woman then walks off in to the crowd, the reflection of Mrs Morgan changes back to the reflection of the homeless woman as if Mrs Morgan's spirit had left the body of the homeless woman.

Sally cannot wait for tomorrow, pest control are coming tomorrow. Sally has just come back from town, she starts putting the shopping away, she notices more cockroach excrement in the cupboards and even the fridge, she cleans the whole of the kitchen including the fridge, "that is nasty" she says to herself as she cleans up the mess left by the cockroaches. The kitchen is now spotless, she puts the fruit she bought from town in to the fruit bowl and goes to pick the children up from school, it's another dull rainy day so Sally runs to the car.

After forty five minutes she arrives home with the children as soon as she enters the house she is confronted by the sight of a cockroach, she kills it but there are three more on the way to her kitchen, she kills them all and puts the remains in the rubbish when she notices the fruit bowl is empty apart from the small remains of fruit and cockroaches, Sally picks up the fruit bowl up and throws in the rubbish outside, she opens the fridge, cockroaches are everywhere, "oh my god" she gasps, the cockroaches are all over the living room, the kitchen and the downstairs of the house, she orders Mandy and Jason to go upstairs.

The children go upstairs to their bedrooms, Sally phones Dan, he answers, she tells him about the cockroaches "I have told the kids not to go downstairs for anything, we are staying upstairs tonight" she explains, Dan tells her he will be back home at dinner time tomorrow, "what time are pest control coming out?" he asks, "they said they would be here between one and two o'clock" she answers, "ok" Dan says, "I will try to get back in time to see them" he adds, "has anyone else seen or had dreams about Mrs Morgan?" he asks, "not to what I know! answers Sally, "why?" she asks, "nothing, it's just, nothing" Dan answers, Sally knows something is wrong, "I will talk to you later" he says and abruptly ends the call, leaving Sally wondering what is going on. Its dark, cold and windy outside Justin walks in to the house, "mom, Jason, Clare" he shouts as the walks through the hallway killing any cockroach in his path, "we're up here son" he hears his mom shout back, later that night; everyone in the house is sleeping.

It is 3.03 am and Dan is sleeping in a hotel called the Ram, when he hears a voice, "Daniel" the voice says "follow me" the voice whispers Dan looks up, its Mrs Morgan, she is walking out of his hotel room, he gets out of bed and follows her, when Dan leaves the hotel room he is surprised to see that he is by the standing stones outside Crudes Castle, he sees the same hooded figures that were witnessed by Justin, Dan looks at Mrs Morgan and notices that she is looking at something in the distance, he turns to see what she could be looking at, when he sees Sally walking towards the standing stones, he walks towards her, "what are you doing here?" he asks, Sally carries on walking in a trance like state, "Mrs Morgan is going to show me something, something I need to see" she answers calmly, Dan turns around to ask Mr Morgan why she has bought them here, Mrs Morgan points to the standing stones, the hooded men are chanting a repetitive almost hypnotic chant, Sally and Dan watch as children are taken to the centre of the stones, they witness a graphic, cruel and satanic human sacrifice ritual, Sally begins to cry, Dan looks at Mrs Morgan "you must leave, your house for the sake of your children, for the sake of the local people and for the sake of your souls" Mr Morgan explains, she seems very weak and fragile as she speaks "I am not leaving" Dan insists, "it's my fucking house" he adds, Mr Morgan starts twitching, Dan and Sally watch her as her twitching gets worse by the second and she begins foaming at the mouth, weak and almost lifeless she grabs Dan by the right arm, scratching him with her nails and drawing blood "the spirits of 13 Crudes Castle are awakening" she looks at Dan and she coughs up huge amounts of blood and slimy mucus, she just about manages to get one last sentence out "there is a terrible curse in your home" she cries, she begins to cough again, this time some of the blood and mucus she has coughed up lands on Dan's arm, she still has a tight grip, Dan sets himself free and wipes the blood from his arm, causing Mrs Morgan to drop the floor with a huge bang, the bang wakes Dan and Sally they are miles apart yet having the same dream at the same time.

Dan is now lying in bed wide awake, he is thinking of his dream as is Sally, he feels a burning sensation on his right arm, he takes his arm from beneath the blanket and looks at it, he is amazed to see that he has four scratches, scratches that were caused by Mrs Morgan grabbing his arm in his dream, they are bleeding and they feel very sore, Dan opens up the first aid box in his hotel room he puts antiseptic on the scratches he then goes to bed, he struggles to sleep in his cold hotel room. The next day comes, its 7.00 am and Dan's alarm on his mobile phone wakes him, Dan feels very tired as he hardly slept, he has a few things to do before starting his journey home, Dan rushes to get himself ready to go to the office, by ten o'clock Dan starts the journey home. After half an hour of driving Dan is feeling tired, his eye lids are feeling heavy, Dan is driving on a long stretch of dual carriageway, all of a sudden the place goes dark as if a storm is coming, Dan turns up the radio in the hope it will help him stay awake. After singing along to one of his favourite songs Dan notices it get darker still, he turns his lights on when something on the side of the road catches his eye. It's a man in a black hooded robe, it reminds Dan of his dream, he turns his head to have a look as he drives past him, and the figure stays perfectly still. Dan turns his head to face the road when he sees another figure standing directly in front of him, "oh shit" Dan shouts at the top of his voice as he slams on his breaks, the car speeds towards the hooded figure, Dan notices the inside of his robe is red, the hooded figure looks up straight in to Dan's eyes, Dan feels fear like he has never felt it before as the bright red demonic eyes are staring at him, he closes his eyes and screams.

Upon reopening his eyes Dan is amazed to see that he is still alive, he looks in his mirror and sees no sign of the hooded figure anywhere, he notices that its now bright and quite sunny "what the fuck happened then" Dan asks himself, he decides that he must have fallen to sleep at the wheel, upon deciding this Dan thinks that it would probably be best if he stops at a service station and gets himself a coffee. Meanwhile at the house Sally has taken the children to school and she is now waiting for pest control by now the cockroaches are all over the house, they have completely taken over the downstairs, centipedes, spiders, slugs and snails are also in the house, Sally is exhausted like Dan she has had trouble sleeping after her dreams, Justin walks downstairs, "oh my days" he says as he looks around the house, Sally looks at Justin "where could they be coming from?" she asks, "I dunno" Justin answers "but I am out of here" he adds before walking out the house, slamming the door on the way.

Sally is upstairs tidying Mandy's bedroom when the door knocks she looks at the time and sees its 12.46pm, she runs to the door hoping that it is pest control, its Mr and Mrs Morgan, Sally tells them there is a fault with their gas, she tells them "it is best for you not to enter, for your own safety" Dan pulls up and gets out of the car, Sally notices he looks tired, he walks up to Thomas and shakes his hand "how's Mrs Morgan?" Dan asks, Thomas takes his hat off and holds it to his chest, Shelly looks at the floor, "she's dead" Thomas answers, Dan and Sally look at each other "I am so sorry to hear that" Sally tells them, "when did she die?" she asks, "they found her this morning lifeless in her bed" Shelly answers, "but what was strange was she had broken two broken arms, a broken leg and cuts and bruises all over her yet no signs that she had got up in the night" Thomas adds, "that is strange" Dan mutters quietly, Thomas looks at Dan "something else is very strange" Thomas tells him "she had something in her hand" Thomas puts his hand in his pocket and pulls out a photograph, he hands it to Dan, it's a photograph of a business card, the business card for the Ram Hotel in Birmingham, "why would she have this in her hand?" Thomas asks, Sally looks over at Dan, "you are from Birmingham" Thomas points out, "have you ever heard of the ram hotel?" he asks, Dan shakes his head "no, sorry" Dan answers, his wife is now staring at Dan intensely "where is the card now?" Dan asks, Thomas explains that the police took it for analysis, "they do not believe it to be murder but they have to investigate due to the cuts and bruises" Dan notices Shelly is looking at him he looks back sees her staring at the scratches on his arm, he quickly tries to cover the scratches but it's too late she has already seen them.

After talking for a bit longer the Morgan's leave, it's now half past one and Sally is concerned that pest control may not turn up, Dan walks in to the house, "oh my goodness" he gasps as he looks around at the insects that have now taken over his house, Sally quickly walks up to him "what is going on?" she asks, "I had a dream last night" she tells him Dan looks at her "I dreamt it to" he says, "do you think I killed Mrs Morgan?" he asks, "I dropped her in the dream, I stayed at the Ram Hotel and I seen her there" Sally looks at Dan "why did you tell them that you have never heard of the Ram Hotel?" she asks, "I was scared" Dan answers, the door knocks abruptly ending the conversation.

Chapter 8. Infestation.

Sally opens the door she is happy to see it is pest control, "hello Mr and Thomson is it?" he asks, "yes" Sally answers, "thank goodness you are here" she adds, she invites them in "my name is Derek and this is my assistant Clive" he looks around, "oh my" he gasps, "when did the problem start?" he asks, Sally explains that they had the problem "pretty much as soon as they had moved in to the house, but the problem has rapidly worsened over the last week" Clive and Derek look around in amazement, "this looks bad, we are going to need a empty house, for at least a week, it looks like a bad infestation" Derek tells them, "we could stay at my mom's" Dan tells Sally. Derek and Clive continue looking around the house "we need all food taken out of the house, with an infestation like this we are going to have to try chemicals, baits and boric acid, after an hour of looking around the house Derek and Clive hands Dan a business card with the quoted price written on it, they walk out the door "think about it and let us know" Derek advises.

Sally shuts the door "what know?" she asks, Dan hands her the quote, Sally looks at the card "three thousand five hundred pound" she gasps at the price, "what are we going to do" she asks, Dan is thinking about it, "fuck it, I will do it myself" he says, "I know what I need to do and I can use the internet for tips, you will have to take the kids to your moms, Justin can stay here and give me a hand" he says, Sally does not really want to stay with Dan's parents but she knows she has no choice as the house is in no condition for the children and chemicals will be used, Sally tells Justin the news, "that's not fair" Justin whines, "you know what's not fair?" Dan replies as he walks up to Justin "your now eighteen, you do not work and you do not pay board so the least you can do is shut up complaining and lend me a hand" Justin agrees "besides I will pay you" Dan adds, Justin smiles.

Later that day Sally, Mandy, Jason and Clare are packing some clothes ready for the journey, Clare is walking down the stairs with a huge suitcase, Justin sees her and shouts "fucking hell, Clare you are only going for a week" Clare orders him to "shut up" everyone is ready to go and Dan has arranged it with his parents, they say their goodbyes and get in the car, "I will phone you in an hour" Dan tells Sally, "see you soon, love you" Sally says and then she blows Dan a kiss, as soon as they leave Dan gets in to his car and drives to a huge DIY store, he gets all sort of poisons, traps, boric acid and many different household cleaning products, he also stops of at his local shop and picks up some cold meats, fruit and other foods to try as baits, by the time Dan gets home it's starting to get dark, Dan phones Sally to make sure she made it to his moms safely and then he and Justin begin to put down the poison and the traps, "we have to find where they are coming from" Dan tells Justin, "mom said she thinks they are coming from the back of the units in the kitchen" Justin replies, after only ten minutes they have already killed a few dozen cockroaches. Dan looks at the back of the units in the kitchen, he sees it's very damp and there are cockroaches under the unit, Dan and Justin take out the unit and the fridge freezer to see what is underneath it.

When Justin and Dan are moving the unit they disturb hundreds of cockroaches they are everywhere and they are huge, Justin steps back holding on to the unit when he feels something moving on him he looks down at himself only to see cockroaches and other insects all over him, he screams, Dan quickly looks at Justin he sees the cockroaches on him, he sees the panic in Justin's face and starts laughing, Justin quickly knocks them off him, "that is disgusting" he moans, "oh man up a bit" his dad advises "you probably just disturbed a nest" he adds.

Dan starts inspecting the wall behind the kitchen unit, its black with mould and the plaster is soft to touch, there is an hole at the bottom of the wall, Dan kicks it with his steel toe cap boot, the plaster drops of the wall easily and the hole gets a little bigger, Dan kicks it again this time a huge group of insects are disturbed and run in to the kitchen, Dan kills a few by stamping on the but the insects are everywhere, Dan looks at Justin and says "I think we have found where they are coming from son, I will go and get a hammer for access" he walks out of the kitchen. Justin looks at the hole he has a strange feeling of déjà vu,

Dan walks back in the kitchen with an hammer, he walks to the wall ready to knock it down when Justin stops "what are you going to do?" Justin asks, "what if the ceiling falls on us?" he adds, Dan looks at the wall, "it only lath and plaster and its rotten, it's got to go" the plaster is soft and damp with a very strong odour, Dan looks through the hole he has created, "there could be extra room here" he reveals, Justin looks in, the hole is black with darkness, "get me a torch" Dan ask as he carries on knocking the wall down.

Chapter 9. Hole

Justin starts looking at the hole, suddenly he remembers his hallucination, he remembers that he has seen this hole before, "I have seen this before" he tells his dad, Dan is baffled by this claim, "how have you seen this before?" he asks, "when I was hallucinating, I seen the kitchen but the kitchen looked different, it was set out different and it was dirty, dusty and greasy" Justin stops talking and begins to think, Dan begins to work on the wall again "them drugs really fucked with your head didn't they?" Dan claims Justin is still thinking then he talks about his hallucination "I remember, there was an old lady with white hair she looked weak, she looked like she was dying" Dan stops working and looks at Justin "she told me not to go down there" Justin starts thinking again, acting almost as if he is in a trance, "and then what?" Dan asks, Justin snaps out of his trance like state "I donno" Justin answers "after that all I remember is lying on the floor looking up at my mom and Clare" he adds. Dan starts working on the wall again, after an hour and half the wall had been completely removed, they are tidying up the mess, "where is the torch?" Dan asks Justin hands him the torch over. Dan slowly walks in to the new room, the room itself is very small but Dan notices some stairs, "oh my god" he gasps, "what? Justin asks, "We have a cellar" Dan answers, Justin is again reminded of his hallucination. "Are you coming down" Dan asks, Justin enters the dark room its very cold, they both start cautiously, slowly walking, they get to the top of the stairs, "stay close and we can both use the torch" Dan orders, but Justin uses the light from his mobile phone instead, they carry on walking down the steps, when suddenly the torch stops working "shit" Dan gasps, "must be the battery, come on we will have to use your light to get back" he says, but then Justin's phone turns off, "the battery was full" Justin insists, he tries to turn it on again, but the phone will not turn on.

Justin and Dan are now standing on the stairs in complete darkness, they cannot see a thing, "what we going to do now?" Justin asks, "Get out of here, walk towards the light" Dan answers they start to feel their way up the steps. In complete darkness they climb a few steps, Dan feels like he has something crawling on him but he is more concerned with getting out of the darkness for now, upon getting out of the darkness and in to the kitchen Dan looks at Justin and Justin looks at Dan, they are both covered with insects and dirt from feeling the walls, they quickly shake them off "we will have a look down there in the morning when its daylight, and with a torch" Dan says, Justin agrees. The cold from the cellar is making the whole house feel cold, "come on" Dan orders he walks to the garage, Justin follows, "what are you doin?" Justin asks, Dan walks to the back of the garage and drags out an eight foot by four foot piece of plywood, "this should stop the draught for tonight" Dan explains, they take it in to the kitchen and cover the hole, the plywood comfortable covers the hole, its 10.30 pm "do you want a beer?" Dan asks, Justin thinks about it "no thank you" he answers, "I am going to bed" he adds, and he walks upstairs.

Dan looks at the traps and he sees that they have caught thousand of cockroaches and the poison would have killed even more Dan believes he may have solved the cockroach problem and saved a fortune at the same time, the room seems empty of living cockroaches. Dan puts some more traps and poison down and goes upstairs, Justin is already sleeping and Dan is now getting ready for bed, he brushes his teeth and gets in to his bed.

Dan feels like he has only been in bed for two minutes when he hears something, he starts to listen carefully but the sound stops Dan lays back down and starts to relax when he hears the sound again, he sits up on the edge of his bed, he hears a chanting noise, the noise sounds familiar to Dan but he cannot think where he may of heard before, until it hits him, he heard it in his dream, the same dream in which he killed Mrs Morgan, he rushes to the window and look towards the standing stones "what is going on?" he asks himself, he can still hear the sound of chanting and although he cannot see the standing stones from his window he sees a glow in the distance, he believes there may have a fire lit.

Meanwhile Justin is also sleeping when the chanting wakes him, he looks at his phone to see the time it is 3.22am, he tries to get back to sleep and ignore the chanting but the chanting is too loud, Justin stands up, he walks to his window and looks outside, he does not see anything unusual but the chanting continues, Justin also recognizes the strange hypnotic chant and he remembers where he heard from, Justin has a bad feeling, as he walks back to his bed, he has a feeling that someone is watching him, he looks around the room and then looks at the window that's when he sees something but not through the window in the reflection of the window, it's the old lady he seen when he was hallucinating. She is in the reflection Justin rushes towards the door to get out of the bedroom, when something catches his eye in the mirror,

Justin looks at the mirror and sees her again, she walks up the mirror, Justin can see her lips moving but he hears no sound, he runs out of the room and in to the hallway.

Dan is still looking out of the window when the chanting comes to an abrupt end, Dan moves away from the window when something in the mirror catches his eye, he quickly turns on the light and looks again, when he sees his reflection, he steps closer and sees the reflection is showing his hands covered in blood, he moves away from the mirror and looks at his hands the blood is not there. Dan slowly looks in the mirror again this time he sees Mrs Morgan staring back at him, Dan runs out of the bedroom and in to the hallway where he sees Justin, "what is going on?" gasps Justin, Dan is finding it hard to catch his breath after doing so he answers "I don't know but I am getting out of here" they start walking very quickly down the stairs when they hear banging "what is that noise?" Dan whispers, they slowly walk to the kitchen as Dan passes the mirror Dan and Justin see the blood on Dan's hands through the reflection, Justin is about to scream but before he gets the chance he vanishes without a trace, Dan watches in absolute terror "Justin" he shouts there is no reply, "Justin" he screams at the very top of his voice, the banging continues right upon until he enters the kitchen, it then stops. Dan slowly walks up to the plywood, he moves the cupboards that are either side of the plywood and holding the plywood in to place, it is cold and pitch black but there does not seem to be anyone there until Dan hears something, it seems to be getting closer and then he hears something slowly walking up the stairs, "who is it?" Dan shouts, "Is that you Justin? He adds, there is no answer the walking continues, he sees a figure in the hole, "Justin is that you?" Dan asks again, he picks up the hammer ready to defend himself if need be, the figure steps out of the darkness, he sees glowing red eyes on an evil demonic looking face, the next thing that Dan remembers is waking up, Dan quickly gets out of bed and looks in the mirror the blood has gone from his hands, he quickly runs in to Justin's room, Justin is not there, "Justin" he shouts, "what" he hears coming from downstairs, Dan walks down, Justin is eating breakfast cereal, Dan is relieved to say the least.

Dan walks in to the kitchen "how come you are up this early?" he asks, "I couldn't sleep" Justin replies "not after the dreams I was having last night" he adds, "the old woman in the mirror and the fucked up ritual?" Dan guesses Justin stops eating "how do you?" Justin asks, "I dreamt it to!" Dan answers; Justin looks back at his dad and asks, "How?" Dan shrugs his shoulders "I don't know" Dan answers "but I am pretty sure it’s got something to do with Mrs Morgan" he adds, suddenly the door knocks Dan opens the door, its two police officers "we are looking for a Mr Daniel Thomson" Dan looks surprised "I am he" he answers "come in" he adds. The police officers walk in to the house "excuse the mess, we have a bit of an insect infestation" explains Dan, the older of the two police officers steps forward "My name is Detective Mark Green and this is my colleague Constable George Jones, I do not wish to waste your time so I will be as quick as I can and I will get straight to the point" he says, the police officers explain how Mrs Morgan was found in bed with a severely bruised face and broken bones "despite no sign of forced entry and no one seen entering or leaving the premises on the caring homes CCTV footage" Dan and Justin listen to the story "what does this have to do with me?" Dan asks interrupting Detective Mark Green, the younger police officer pulls out a photograph from his pocket, "she was holding a business card, a business card from the Ram inn hotel in Birmingham, when my work colleagues contacted this hotel the hotel manager told them that you have recently stayed at the hotel" Dan nods his head "I was staying there the night she died, I have no idea how she got that card but it had nothing to do with me" Dan angrily explains "is that all?" he adds Detective Mark Green walks to the front door "that is all for now, thank you for your time" he opens the door and walks out he is followed by his colleague.

The police officers walk to their car and get in, Mark Green does not attempt to drive, he simply sits in the car thinking, his colleague looks at him "what now?" he asks, Mark Green starts the car "I don't know" he sighs "It looks like it will be added to long list of mysteries and secrets that these village holds after all we got nothing on Mr Thomson, we got nothing on anyone" he adds.

Chapter 10. Darkness

Dan is watching the police officers sitting in their car through his living room window, after five minutes he watches the police officers car drive off, Justin is looking at the traps and poison set for the cockroaches, "we have killed thousands of them" he tells he dad with a smile on his face, Justin hears the door slam, he looks through the window and sees his dad rushing in to his car. Sally is still at Dan's parents, Dan's parents have gone out shopping with Clare and Jason, Sally is in the house with Mandy "when are we going home mommy?" Mandy asks, "hopefully very soon" Sally answers as she reads a message on her mobile phone, the message reads, the cockroach extermination going very well, smiley face, Sally is glad to hear it.

After a couple of hours Dan gets back to the house "Justin" he shouts as he enters the house, "what?" Justin shouts back, he is sitting in the living room watching the television "I have an electrician coming out to get some power in the cellar" Dan excitedly explains, he should be here in the next hour, "is this the electrician" Justin asks as a van pulls up on their drive "yes, his name is Dave" Dan answers.

Dave the electrician walks in to the house, Dan and Justin move the plywood "it started with a cockroach infestation, trying to find where the cockroaches were coming from led to me and my son finding a cellar" Dan explains as Dan, Dave and Justin look in to the darkness. Dave goes to his van and gets some temporary lighting to put in, using a torch each Dan and Dave slowly enter the dark hole and start walking down the stairs, Dave has plugged the temporary lighting in to the mains, Justin has waited at the top of the stairs, his job is to wait until he gets the go ahead and turn the mains on, after Dave has set up the lighting, they get to the bottom step they start looking around the place Dan and Dave shine their torches a round "this place looks huge" Dave gasps with amazement, he starts setting up the temporary lighting Dave is looking around the cellar, there is old toys, old newspapers, books, furniture and pieces of junk everywhere.

After ten minutes Dan shouts to Justin "turn the lights on" Justin turns on the lights and the cellar is lit up, "wow" gasps Dan, "its huge" he adds as he looks around, Dave is also looking round there are dead insects on the floor and even a few rats, Justin enters the cellar "oh my god" he gasps, "what do you want, some light and a few electric boxes down here?" Dave asks Dan, "yeah, that would be fine, if you could" Dan replies, Dave looks around "no problem at all" he says as he walks up the stairs and goes to the van to get some tools for the job, Dan walks to the stairs and asks Justin "do you want to grab a bite" Justin follows him "yeah I am starving" they explain to Dave that they will be in a couple of hours, Dave walks down the cellar and starts doing his work.

After three and half hours of working Dave decides to call it a day he walks up the stairs and in to the kitchen. Dan and Justin have gone out to get some rat poison and other cleaning materials, Dan is planning on giving the cellar a good clean, by the time Justin and Dan get back home Dave the electrician has already left, Justin turns on the temporary lighting and they go down the cellar to start cleaning, they set traps for the rats and for the cockroaches, there were still a few cockroaches crawling round the place but Dan could see that the poison and the traps were killing them off quickly and by removing all other food from the house the cockroaches were drawn to the bait. The cellar is a mess there are old newspapers, letters, ornaments, toys and many other strange objects everywhere unfortunately most of the ornaments and toys are broke and most of the old newspapers and letters have been ruined by the damp but many are salvageable, Dan picks up an newspaper that is not bad condition, he walks closer to the light in order to read "this newspaper is from 1919" he tells Justin, Justin is busy looking at an old fashioned puppet, "cool" gasps Justin. "All the stuff that looks unsalvageable can be put outside for now, we will get a skip here tomorrow, the rest we will put somewhere that it will not get damaged" Dan plans, Justin is looking through boxes, there are boxes everywhere "it all appears to be shit" Justin tells his dad. After a few hours of working and looking through boxes of old broken toys, ornaments, old beer bottles and wine bottles Justin looks at the time "its eight o clock" he tells Dan "shall we leave it for now and come back tomorrow" Dan thinks about it, he is feeling tired and still has a few other jobs to do so he agrees "I will order a skip for tomorrow" he says as he looks around the cellar, "hopefully Dave would have the electrics finished by tomorrow" he adds, they go upstairs and place the plywood in front of the hole.

Dan takes some of the old newspapers upstairs with him after cleaning out the cockroach traps and setting new traps, he believes that the cockroach infestation is dying down, something that Dan is very happy about, Justin and Dan phone for a pizza and by half past nine they are eating, after eating his pizza Dan puts some pizza in a trap using it as bait and then he goes to bed leaving Justin downstairs watching television. After twenty minutes of flicking through the channels Justin finally decides that there is nothing on worth watching on the television and turns the television off. He is about to go to bed when he looks at the box of newspapers that his dad had bought up from the cellar, he notices an headline and a small article, the headline reads, "Double murder at Crudes Castle" Justin reads the story of two women that were murdered in June 1915 at Crudes Castle, the newspaper article talks of "ritualistic murders" and the article claims that the crimes were "probably committed by practicing Satanists, members of the occult or a secret society" the article goes on to state that "the police have very few leads to follow and so far there are no suspects." Justin puts the newspaper down and picks up a different one, this one is from November 1st 1917, this time the main headline reads, "Teenage girl missing" Justin carries on reading and discovers a teenager called Mary King was last seen by her friend outside the Red Dragon, she was walking to her house no more than one hundred meters from the pub, her parents waited up until 4.30 am unfortunately she never made it home, Justin looks through five more newspapers each newspaper containing articles on missing people or murders in Crudes castle, he then picks another old newspaper up, as he picks up the old newspaper an old photograph falls to the floor, he picks the photograph up off the floor and looks at the photograph, the photograph is a picture of two men dressed in suits Justin looks at the back of the photograph, written on the back in ink is Henry Cohens and Charles Cooper July 1919, Justin looks at the photograph again, the A4 photo shows Henry

Cohens and Charles Cooper standing by a Rolls Royce Phianna Limo, behind them he sees part of Crudes Castle and three trees, something about the photograph does not feel right but Justin cannot put his finger on what it is.

Justin looks at the time, he sees that it is getting late and he goes to bed and straight to sleep. Next thing Justin knows is, it's dark and he cannot find the light switch, he cannot see anything other than darkness and black, he feels the wall desperately trying to find the light switch, he notices that the walls feel different to the walls in his bedroom "help" he shouts, but there is no reply from anyone, he is alone, Justin sees a light, he walks towards it, then he hears chanting, suddenly the place lights up, he notices that he is in the cellar he is about to find away to get out when he hears something, it sounds like footprints walking towards him, Justin runs to a corner and hides behind some boxes, "what the fuck is going on" the very quietly asks himself. He notices a six foot stone statue of what appears to be a very old Gargoyle, the Gargoyle has its head slightly turned to the right and seems to be looking right at Justin, this makes him feel uncomfortable and nervous, he quickly runs and hides at the other side of the statue, behind more boxes and an old desk Justin watches as an hooded figure walks through the cellar followed by another one and another one, Justin cowers behind the boxes "shit, fuckin shit" he whispers to himself in a huge panic, he then peeps his head over the boxes, he sees there are five hooded figures standing in a circle chanting very strange chants with a small fire in the middle of them, it looks to Justin as if they are worshipping the statue. Justin quickly hides again, he knocks a pile of paper off a desk, papers scatters all over the stone floor, and he sees the hooded figures turn around but he is sure that they have not seen him. He sits and waits for forty seconds before peeping his head over the boxes again to take another look, this time the hooded figures are not standing in a circle, they are standing in a line and they are all looking at Justin, their faces are not human, they are ugly and evil looking, they look like demons they is a strong smell of burning rubber the smell is giving Justin an headache, Justin then looks at the statue, the statue is also staring right at him Justin screams for help as one of the hooded figures tries to grab him, Justin wakes up screaming, he is again in complete darkness, feeling the walls for a light switch "help" he screams at the top of his voice "help" he screams again. A door opens and the light is turned on by Justin's dad, "what the fuck is going on?" Dan asks, Justin is dripping with sweat, Dan asks Justin if he "would like a drink" Justin answers no I need to sleep and he lies on his bed.

Its mid day and Justin is still in bed when he wakes up he hears his dad talking to someone on the phone "I will see you later, love you" Dan says before hanging up "how are you?" he asks, Justin sits on the sofa "I am ok" he answers "since having that acid I have the most crazy dreams" he tells his dad, Dan pours them both a cup of tea, suddenly a huge bang from the cellar disturbs them, "what the fuck is that?" Justin asks with fear in his voice, "Dave" Dan shouts, "sorry" Dave shouts back "I dropped a roll of cable" he adds. Dan goes down to the cellar to explain that he was going out "I will be back at about four" Dan tells the electrician, "I will only be another hour and half" Dave tells him, Dan hands him an envelope with the money for the job in it "lock up as you leave please" Dan asks as he walks to the stairs "I will" Dave answers, he carries on working.

Chapter 11. Little shop of Magik

Justin and Dan go to the nearest town, first they go to an Indian restaurant and have a meal and a couple of drinks, they then have a look around the town, its market day and the town is very busy, Dan buys some tinned food he tells Justin "I can only buy tinned food because of the cockroaches" Justin is deep in thought and not really listening, suddenly Dan sees a strange looking shop, he walks in Justin follows him without really paying attention to where he is going, the shop is called "little shop of magik" and the shop has many strange objects. The shop sells things like Voodoo dolls, Dream catchers, Ouija boards, books on the occult, Pagan rituals, Wicca, Satanism and magic spells, tarot cards and many other weird objects from the occult. Dan walks up to the counter and rings the bell "what are you doing?" asks Justin, an old man walks in from the back of the shop. he looks at Justin and Dan, "can I help you" he asks, Dan smiles and asks "do you have anything that would get rid of ghosts" the old man turns his head to look at Dan "I may have something" he replies, "what sort of ghost are we dealing with?" the old man asks, "I dunno" Dan answers "she must be a witch or something" the old man looks confused "a witch and a ghost are two very different things" he says, Dan explains that this "ghost" was haunting them before she died, "she was controlling our dreams as she lay dying in a care home, but since she died the dreams have not gone away" the old man starts messing with something behind the counter, he pulls out a bag of stones, "these stones have the power to repel spirits of the dead" the old man claims, Dan looks at the stones, the stones are black and they shine "how much are they?" Dan asks "fifty pounds" the old man replies, Dan offers the old man forty pounds after a quick think the old man accepts it, Dan and Justin leave the shop with the stones.

As they leave the shop Justin begins to laugh and mock Dan "what you laughing at?" Dan asks, Justin takes the stones from his dad "you do know that you have just been ripped off, don't you?" Justin asks "I mean forty pound for a few shiny bricks, you must be mad" he adds, Dan takes the stones back from Justin "forty pound would be a absolute bargain if it works" Dan answers, "and if it don't work I will give them your Nan and granddad as a Christmas present" he adds, Justin laughs.

Meanwhile at Dan's parent's house Sally is struggling to see eye to eye with Dan's parents and in particularly Dan's mom. Dan parents are Clive and Margret Thomson, Clive was a very successful business man, Clive started the family business in 1979 and retired from it in 2009 leaving Dan in charge, Dan started working for the business from the age of twenty, Clive Thomson and Margret Thomson are both in their late sixties, they live in a huge mansion, Sally believes that Dan's mother looks down on her as Sally is from a poor family, she was brought up on a council estate. Sally is pretty desperate to go home but she knows she can't, Clare, Jason and Mandy are more than happy to stay longer as they love staying at their grandparents. After having another petty argument with Margret, Sally goes upstairs and lays on the bed that she has been sleeping in, "I cannot wait to get home" she says to herself, she picks up her phone and starts writing a text to Dan.

Dan and Justin are now nearly home, Dan receives a text message he reads it "I think your mom might be back home by tomorrow" he tells Justin, they pull up outside the house, much to Dan's surprise the electricians van is still outside, "that's weird" Dan says to Justin, "he said he was nearly finished" he adds, they walk in to the house, "Dave" Dan shouts, there is no reply, Dan walks closer to the cellar "Dave" he shouts again, again there is no answer, Dan hears music playing in the cellar and he assumes that Dave cannot hear him shouting over the music so Dan walks down to the cellar "Dave" he shouts, Dan looks around and all the new electrics seem to be fitted and working, but still no sign of Dave, Dan turns on the light at the far end of the cellar, when he discovers Dave hanging room the ceiling "shit" Dan shouts, he falls over trying to get away from Dave's hanging body. Dan runs up the stairs to call the police, it does not take long for the police to get there, after hours of looking around it becomes obvious to the police that Dave had committed suicide, at twenty past midnight the police and forensics are finally finished, Dan decides not to tell Sally anything about what happened to Dave the electrician "I will have to make her stay at my parents for at least one more night" he tells Justin. Dan walks over to the bags of shopping that he bought hours before, he starts putting the tinned food in the cupboard, Justin and Dan notice there are no living cockroaches in sight though the traps are still full of dead ones, Dan finds the bag of stones, he puts them on a window sill Dan and Justin go around the house cleaning the traps out and putting more poison down.

Its 1.30 am before Dan goes to bed; Justin goes to bed at 2.00 am. The next day Dan wakes up at 8.00am he had a night with no nightmares for the first time in a while, he goes downstairs and phones his wife, Sally picks up the phone, he tells Sally about the cellar and the suicide, Sally is gobsmacked "oh my god" she gasps, Dan tells her to stay at his parents for at least a couple of more days, Sally reluctantly agrees, "how are the kids" Dan asks, "Jason and Clare are fine" Sally answers, "Mandy is having bad dreams again" she adds, "she told me she had been dreaming about Mrs Morgan last night, she wakes up sweating and screaming" Sally explains, Dan tells Sally everything will be better when she gets home "how can you be so sure?" Sally asks, to which Dan answers "I have a feeling."

Justin stays in bed until nearly midday, when he finally gets up Dan has already been working for hours cleaning out the cellar, Justin goes down to see his dad, "Dracula has awoken" Dan Jokes, Justin sarcastically laughs, Dan has nearly finished cleaning, "give me a hand putting these boxes in the skip" he asks, Justin and Dan start carrying the rubbish up the stairs and in to the skip, Justin asks his dad if he had read any of the newspapers that he had salvaged "no, why?" Dan asks, Justin tells Dan that they all contain stories of local ritual murders, Dan laughs, "What you think that the area is full of devil worshippers, wizards and witches?" Dan asks with a huge grin of his face, "Just read them" Justin tells him, "I will later" Dan answers "I am working at the moment, unlike you" he adds.

After a few hours work they have finally finished cleaning the cellar, "it looks bigger" Justin says as he walks around looking at the place, Dan walks around looking at some of the things that they have salvaged, Justin picks up a newspaper, this one is dated 22nd March 1918, the newspaper has the headline "dead body found at Crudes Castle" the newspaper reports claim the victim was unidentified and the killer was still at large, Justin passes the newspaper to Dan, Dan reads it, "there are loads more" Justin says, Dan starts looking through the newspapers and many of them do have stories of missing people, ritualistic murders and suicides, "that is weird" Dan says, he reads at least six articles all of which talk of missing people, murders and rituals to which he replies "that's how people used to be in the old days, human sacrifice was practiced in Satanism and paganism all over the world but mankind has evolved since them days, that sort of thing does not happen anymore."

Dan and Justin are about to walk upstairs, when Dan notices some of the walls does not look like the other walls, the wall is made of stripes of wood where as the rest are made of stone, Dan taps the wood, "its hollow" he tells Justin, "so what?" Justin replies, Dan pushes against the wood, "there could be another room behind here" Dan excitedly explains, the wood is damp and rotten as Dan puts pressure on the wall, he easily creates a hole, "there is another room in here" he excitedly tells Justin, Dan picks up an hammer and begin to knock a section of the wall down, Justin carries the damp wood from the cellar to the skip, after ten minutes they can finally get in to the room.

Upon entering the new room they turn on their torches and see six empty coffins lined up three each side with a gap in the middle at the far end of the room there is a six foot statue of a evil looking gargoyle, the room is very dusty with cob webs all over it, Justin looks around in amazement "I seen this in my dream the other night" he whispers to his dad, Dan walks up to the statue, "oh my god" he gasps, "this is incredible" Justin looks at the statue "it's horrible" he moans, "what is this place?" Justin asks, Dan walks around looking at the strange symbols on the wall "I don't know" Dan answers "but somebody did not want us to find it" he adds.

After twenty minutes of looking around Dan and Justin walk up the stairs, "do you want a sandwich?" Dan asks his son "no thanks" Justin answers, a text message comes through to Justin phone, Justin reads the message and then looks at his dad "that is my friend Carl Cooper, he lives around the corner" he explains "he wants me to go out for a drink with him tonight, but I don't have no money" Justin adds, Dan looks at Justin "you can have thirty quid and that's it" Justin smiles, "thanks dad" he says as he walks out of the room, "where you going now?" Dan asks, "I am going to have a shower" Justin answers, Dan looks at the time its 6.00pm "looks like I will be cleaning the rest of the cellar on my own" Dan says to himself. He walks down to the cellar, the new room is dark so Dan puts a couple halogen lamps in there to light it up, Dan looks at the statue and smiles "you are an ugly fucker, aren't you" he jokes to himself, he walks up to the statue and puts his hand on its head, Dan gets a strange feeling from doing this, he quickly tries to move his hand, his hand seems to be stuck, he uses his other hand to pull his hand free, after a struggle he manages to free himself, he stands back and looks at the statue again, Dan's heart is racing he holds his chest, he begins to feel a huge buzz from the statue, "what the fuck was that?" he says to himself. Dan hears Justin walk in to the cellar "I am going to the pub now" he tells his dad, Dan gives him the money "I should be back before midnight" Justin says before leaving, Dan walks out of the cellar deciding to wait until Justin is with him.

Dan makes himself a sandwich and a cup of tea, he sits down to watch the news and eat when he hears a huge bang coming from the cellar, he stands up and walks down to the cellar to investigate, when he enters the cellar he cannot see what could have caused the sound, until he walks in to the newly discovered room, one of the coffins has fallen from the stand "how did that happen?" Dan thinks to himself, when he hears someone breathing heavily, Dan starts to listen the breathing sounds close, he looks at the statue, Dan feels freaked out by the statue, he walks from the room as fast as he can, he walks back up the stairs and covers the hole with plywood.

Chapter 12. Lysergic acid diethylamide.

The next day Dan wakes up in his chair he fallen to sleep while waiting for Justin to come home, he looks at his phone for the time, its 7.30 am Dan walks upstairs to Justin's room to make sure he got back safely, to Dan's shock and horror Justin is not in his room, he quickly phones Justin's mobile, the phone goes straight to answer machine "where are you, call me as soon as you get this?" Dan leaves on a message he notices a noise coming from outside the house, it’s a moaning noise "Justin, is that you?" he shouts, Dan hears coughing as if someone is spewing, he walks outside to see Justin lying on the floor in his own vomit "what happened son?" he asks, Justin does not answer, Dan carries him in to the house and lays him on the sofa, "I am going to find out what happened" he says as he walks out of the living room leaving Justin who is now sleeping on the sofa. Dan gets in to his car and drives to Carl Cooper’s house, when he gets to the house Dan notices they have a stone gargoyle that looks very similar to the statue in his cellar, the gargoyle is sitting on the roof of the house and is looking straight at Dan, the gargoyle makes Dan feel uncomfortable, Dan gets a strange feeling that he is being watched, Dan hears a voice in his head, it’s a voice that Dan does not seem to have any control of "I can help you" the voice says Dan looks at the gargoyle, he is getting more and more convinced that the gargoyle is watching him.

Dan gets to the front door of the Cooper’s house and bangs it very loudly, the Cooper’s dog starts barking at him, Carl’s dad (George Cooper) answers the door, he looks at Dan and asks "can I help you?" Dan tries to look behind George but there is nobody there "I would like to have a word with your son please" Dan says, George steps outside the house and shuts the door behind him "what is this involving?" George Cooper asks, Dan looks through the window and sees George Cooper’s wife looking at him, she looks worried "I want to know what happened to my son last night" Dan tells George "your son was with him" he adds, Carl steps outside the house, "It was not me, Mr Thomson" Carl cries, "it was John Jackson and his friends they drugged him" he adds, Dan sees Carl crying and he believes what he tells him, Dan storms off, Carl’s parents give Carl a look of disappointment, Carl walks upstairs and in to his bedroom, Dan gets to the gate and looks back at the house, something looks different, Dan looks again, he notices the gargoyle that looked similar to the statue he found in his cellar is not there, Dan looks around confused, but he is to angry to really think about what just happened.

Dan rushes home when he gets in the house Justin is asleep in his bedroom, Dan quietly shuts the door and walks in to the living room, he picks up the phone and calls his wife, "are you alright?" she asks him, "I'm fine" Dan answers, Dan makes up a lie that they have found a new cockroach nest and it's still not safe for the kids to come back yet, even though the cockroach extermination is going very well, "I cannot stay at your parents much longer" Sally tells Dan, "your mom is doing my head in" she adds, Dan laughs and makes a joke of it, he promises it will be safe for them to come back in a couple of days, Sally goes downstairs and tells Clare, Jason and Mandy "hooray" they cheer Sally is not so happy. "Great" Margret says she smiles at Sally and Sally smiles back.

After the conversation with his wife Dan goes down to the cellar, he walks in to the newly discovered room, he looks around again he is still pretty amazed with what he has found he then looks at the statue, Dan starts clean up the room, throwing away things that appear to be rubbish and keeping other objects, there is an old Ouija board that Dan decides to keep along with a dark mirror used by occultists to look in to the spirit world there are also steel cups used in blood rituals, a collection of old ceremony swords and other weapons, a necklace containing a eye similar to the eye of Horus and many other strange objects, Dan starts cleaning the statue, he wipes the dust and cob webs from it with and with a hard hand brush he begins to scrub it, as he is cleaning he begins to think of Justin and what the local youth have put him through since they have moved, he is angry and the more he thinks of it the angrier he becomes "I am going to get that little bastard for doing that to my son" he says to himself as he cleans the shoulder of the statue, a voice enters his head "bring him to me, bring him to me" the voice starts very faintly but gets louder and louder Dan turns around only to see the statue staring right at him, Dan jumps with a fright and falls to the floor, knocking down a box full of rubbish and banging his head on the way down.

After half an hour laying floor unconscious Dan finally gets to his feet, he has a headache and he can feel a lump on his head but there is no blood much to his relief, Dan looks at the statue again, "what are you?" he gasps, Dan feels terrified when a voice enters his head again "bring him to me, I am revenge" the voice says, Dan can hear it a lot more clear since the bang on his head Dan runs out from the cellar, he still feels confused and hurt from banging his head, he walks upstairs in to Justin's room, Justin is now awake, he is sitting on the edge of his bed "that was horrible" he cries to his dad, his dad sits next to him and says "it was John again, wasn't it?" Justin looks at the floor "yes" he cries. Dan is getting more angry by the minute, how dare he drug by child he thinks to himself, Dan stands up and walks out of the bedroom and down the stairs, he walks down the cellar straight to the statue and says "I will bring him to you" Dan begins to clean the statue again, after forty five minutes Justin walks down the cellar, he walks in the new room, to Justin surprise the statue is spotless, Dan is still cleaning the statue "dad" Justin shouts, his dad looks up, Justin is terrified to see that his dads eye balls appear to be black, Justin screams and covers his face Dan runs up to him "what's wrong, what's wrong?" he asks Justin looks at his dad, he looks in to his eyes they now appear to be normal "what's wrong?" Dan asks again "nothing, I'm fine" Justin answers "I thought the effects had worn off but they obviously have not" he adds Justin looks at the statue "I have got to get out of here" he cries holding his head as he walks out, Dan takes a looks at the statue and follows Justin upstairs "we are going to get him back" Dan tells Justin, Justin looks at his dad "just leave it" Justin says, "he is not worth it" he adds, his dad begins to laugh, "we left it last time and he done it again, this time we can have the fun." Justin walks out of the kitchen in to the living room he sits down on the chair "what you going to do?" Justin asks with a concerned tone to his voice, his dad smiles "just give him and his friends a taste of their own medicine" he puts his hand in his pocket and pulls out three small bottles "what's this? Justin asks, "Lysergic acid diethylamide" Dan answers, "more commonly known as LSD" he adds, they have got a bottle each Dan says as he carries on laughing, and Justin is a bit worried!

Dan begins to explain his plan "tomorrow night I am going to go to the pub and wait for them, I will approach them and start a conversation, they have seen me about but I am pretty sure they do not know that I am your father" Dan starts going in to detail about "the plan" I need to go to town and get some stuff for this, he quickly gets his coat "are you coming" he asks Justin, Justin drops on the chair "nah, I will pass" he answers, Dan walks back toward Justin "this is going to be awesome, you will see" he insists "I am going to teach those little pricks a lesson they will never forget and they will never mess with you again" he adds, he walks to his car and drives off, Justin turns on the TV and starts flicking through the channels "there is never anything on that is worth watching" he moans to himself as he puts on a news channel.

A few hours pass before Dan gets back and when he does he has four strange masks, the type of masks that are used for rituals, they look like venetian masks but they are very twisted, dark and demonic in appearance and two of them have goat horns on them, "we are going to scare the fuck out of these little pricks" he tells Justin, Justin looks at his dad laughing and has big doubts that this is the right thing to do, "I am going to bed now" he tells his dad, "goodnight son" his dad replies, Justin walks upstairs.

The next day comes and Justin wakes up at 11.30 am, he goes in to the kitchen, he feels a lot better but he still has a bit of an headache, Justin looks in the living room expecting to find his dad but his dad is not there, Justin looks outside and sees that Dan's car is still on the drive so he walks down to the cellar, Justin walks in to the newly discovered room only to see Dan cleaning the statue again "what are you doing?" Justin asks, Dan looks up and smiles "I am just cleaning him up a bit" he answers "Justin looks at the statue "you cleaned it yesterday" he says with a slightly concerned tone to his voice "I know" Dan says "I am varnishing it" he adds "whatever" Justin mutters to himself as he goes to walk out of the room, "Justin" Dan shouts "are you ready for tonight?" he asks, Justin is still not up for it, he tries to think of an excuse or a way out "well I still feel a bit" Justin is interrupted "no excuses" Dan states "we are getting them tonight, before your mom gets back" he adds.

Meanwhile Sally is at the park with Mandy, Mandy is happily playing on the swing, Sally looks at her phone and sees she has a message from Clare, the message reads Dinner is nearly done. Sally puts her phone in to her bag and looks up at Mandy, Mandy is waving at someone Sally looks around but there is nobody there "who are you waving at?" Sally asks, Mandy seems to be watching someone behind Sally but Sally still does not see anybody there "who are you waving at" Sally asks again, Mandy turns her head and looks at her mother "Mrs Morgan" she answers, Sally looks confused "you do know that Mrs Morgan is dead, don't you?" Sally asks, Mandy looks at the floor "I know" she answers "but I see her all the time" she explains, Sally picks Mandy up and rushes to the car.

Chapter 13. Justin's Revenge.

Justin and Dan are getting ready to go to the pub and get Justin's revenge, Justin has a bad feeling about the plan and about the mental state of his dad, Dan is still very angry, to angry to think about what he is doing, "I am not doing this" Justin cries, he runs up the stairs, Dan follows him up "listen I will bring them here, you don't even have to leave the house" he explains, Justin stays on his bed and Dan drives to the Red Dragon. Dan parks outside and walks in to the pub, John Jackson, Jack Gould and Anthony Collins are already in the pub they walked in about ten minutes earlier, Dan looks at them and smiles "you are going on a journey to hell tonight" he laughs to himself, Dan over hears the three young men talking, "I need a job" John says to Ant, "I am fucking skint" he adds, "I know that feeling" John replies, Dan walks over to them "did I just hear someone say that they need a job?" he asks, "what's it got to do with you?" John asks "I am the owner of a very large nationwide food distributing company" Dan explains, he hands them his business card, they all recognize his business "man I eat this brand all the time" Jack laughs, Dan smiles "are you interested in a job?" he asks, all three of them reply "yes" "come with me" Dan says, they follow him to his car. "Jump in" instructs Dan, they all jump in "wow, this car is bad ass" Ant gasps looking at the smart interior, Dan drives back, with John Jackson, Jack Gould and Anthony Collins in the car and a huge grin on his face.

When Dan and the others get to the house Dan orders them to wait outside, he rushes in the house, Justin is sitting on the sofa in the living room watching television, "quick get upstairs" Dan tells Justin "I have got them waiting outside" he adds, Justin runs up the stairs "don't do anything you are going to regret" he advises his dad but Dan is still very angry, "the only people that will be regretting anything is them three" Dan laughs, Justin rolls his eyes in despair. Dan goes to the front door "come in, come in" he says politely all three of them walk in to his house, "get the drinks out" John asks, Dan is annoyed by this "fuck you" he thinks to himself as the anger builds up, Dan considers smashing the bottle in John's face but he decides to stick to the plan so he regains his composure and Dan pours them all a very generous shot of whiskey, they all down their drinks, except for Dan, he very quickly pours his drink to a plant pot, John holds his glass out for another, Dan fills his glass and he also fills Jack and Ants glasses, they down the drinks again, Dan pours more to the plant, Dan pours yet another, he walks in to the kitchen and gets the three bottles of Lysergic acid diethylamide, "I am sending you on a journey tonight" he says to himself as he pours dangerous doses in the bottom of each glass, Dan then pulls out a special forty year old whiskey and puts a drop in each glass, he walks out of the kitchen with a huge smile on his face "drink up lads" he orders, John, Jack and Ant are already quite drunk "this is a special drink" Dan smiles as he shows off the bottle and hands out the glasses, "one, two, three" he counts they all down there drinks, this time Dan joins them after all Dan does not waste forty year old whiskey. After they down their drinks Dan sits back in his chair and smiles, he carefully watches them as the Lysergic acid diethylamide begins to takes effect, after five minutes John and Ant start to feeling strange "what is going on" Ant asks, John is staring at one of Sally ornaments intensely "what the fuck are you looking at?" Jack asks "what is happening?" he adds, Dan leaves the room. Dan goes upstairs and tells Justin "they are all downstairs tripping their faces off" Justin cannot believe that his dad has actually gone through with it "time to have some fun" Dan adds.

John, Jack and Ant are downstairs, Dan has left calming, relaxing music on for them to listen to in an attempt to make the atmosphere calm and relaxed for his guests, John and Ant are slouched on the sofa laughing, Jack is sitting on the floor he is also laughing "that whiskey is fucking good" John jokes, suddenly the music changes, Dan has found what he considers to be the scariest, darkest music he can find and added to a playlist, the change in music instantly changes the moods and feelings of John, Jack and Ant, they now feel scared and paranoid "turn this shit off" John demands when the door opens, John, Jack and Ant are horrified to see Justin and Dan wearing the dark and twisted masks and robes, Dan turns the music up louder holding the remote in his hand, John panics and runs to the door, Dan shuts it, "sit down" Dan demands, John quickly sits down. Dan turns his head towards Jack and Ant they both sit down without Dan even saying anything. "Do you know who I am?" Dan asks the three lads, they look at each other "no" Jack answers, Dan laughs "I am the fucking devil and tonight I have come to claim your souls" he shouts, "no" John screams, Dan walks up to John, he picks up a newspaper rolls it up and starts hitting him with it, "shut the fuck up" Dan orders, John lays on the floor crying "stop crying" Dan shouts “stop crying, you fuckin pussy” John stops crying.

Dan looks at John, John is sitting on the floor, he is utterly terrified "I have something to show you" Dan tells them, follow me he instructs, Justin is wearing his mask laughing at what Dan is doing, Dan leads them down to the cellar "wow, what is this place" Ant gasps, Dan laughs and in a deep voice he answers "your worst nightmare, follow me" Dan and Justin led them in to the room that the statue stands in, Justin does not like the statue but he knows that it will freak them out, they look around at the coffins and then Jack notices the statue "what the fuck is that" he gasps, John and Ant look as well "that thing is nasty" Ant gasps, John does not say anything he just looks for a few seconds, Justin walks up to his dad and whispers "that's enough now, isn't it?" Dan laughs again "that's enough?" he repeats "I have not even started with these little scumbags yet" Dan adds.

Dan starts chanting at first Justin joins in and he thinks it is funny, until he notices that Dan is chanting the same chant that Justin has heard when he was having his own hallucinations, he stops chanting and looks up, he sees that Dan is now joined by five hooded men, the hooded men are also chanting, they have created a circle around the three men, John, Jack and Ant are sitting in the middle crying, Justin looks to his left to see that he is a part of the circle as a hooded figure holds him by the hand, he looks to the right and sees a huge hooded figure tightly holding his hand, they are chanting loudly, Dan is still wearing his mask, Dan steps in to the circle, the two hooded figures behind him join hands in order to keep a circle, Justin notices strange symbolism of the floor, "what is going on?" he very quietly gasps to himself, Justin looks around again and tries to break out of the circle, but the hooded figures are holding his hands so tight he cannot break free, Justin looks up at the statue and then at his dad "no" he shouts but Dan does not react, John is sitting in the circle crying like a baby, he also sees the hooded figures, their faces are so horrible that John cannot even look at them, Jack has his eyes closed, he is desperately screaming and he has his arms and legs tied, Ant desperately looks at Justin he sees that Justin does not want no part of this "help" Ant cries but Justin still cannot break free, he tries and tries until one of the hooded figures look at him, the horrible face and strong smell that is coming from them scares Justin, Justin stops the struggle.

Justin looks around for a way to stop what is happening but he cannot find a way, he looks at Dan as Dan picks up a huge sword that was left in the middle of the room "what are you going to do with that" Justin shouts, again there is no reaction from Dan until he quickly turns around and says "come here" to Justin, the hooded dark figures slowly let go of their grip on his hand, Justin and Dan are standing in front of John, Jack and Ant, the figures have now made the statue part of the circle "remove your mask" Dan orders Justin "what?" Justin asks, "you heard" Dan shouts, remove for mask, Justin slowly removes his mask, John looks at Justin and says "listen I am sorry, we were only having a laugh" Jack quickly interrupts "I had nothing to do with that, it was them two" he insists, Ant looks and Justin and simply cries "help us" Justin looks at his dad and goes to walk off when Dan pulls a huge sword from his robes, Justin turns around only to witness his dad cut Anthony Collins head off "fucking hell dad" Justin shouts as he looks at the head laying on the floor, "what are you doing?" he screams at his dad, Justin looks at the statue, Justin believes the statue is smiling at the sight, John and Jack are screaming "help" Dan looks at them both and orders them to "shut the fuck up" again which they do instantly, Justin runs towards his dad and attempts to take the sword from him, but two hooded figures hold him back Dan looks at Jack "your next" he laughs, he swings the sword, Jack screams as Jacks head hits the floor his continues screaming, Dan laughs, he picks up the heads and holds them by their hair in Johns face "not to worry, they are just off their heads" Dan jokes, John looks at the heads as the heads laugh at Dan's joke, Justin vomits all over the floor, his robe and his shirt. Dan drops the heads on the blood covered floor, John watches the heads scream on their way down to the floor and the heads of Jack and Ant argue with each other in front of him after rolling in to each other and banging heads "ouch that fuckin hurt" Jack's head cries out "you made my nose bleed" Ant's head answers "now it's your turn" Dan tells John, "no please" John begs, John looks at Jack and Ant severed heads "cut his head off" Jack's head shouts "off with his head" Ant shouts Dan simply walks up to him swings his sword and cuts John Jacksons head next thing Justin remembers is laying in bed and it is very bright outside Justin looks at the time it is 7.00 am.

As he lays in bed Justin thinks about last night, surely it was a dream he thinks to himself, by the time he gets out of bed and walks downstairs he has convinced himself the whole thing was a dream "alright son" Dan says as Justin enters the kitchen "how did you sleep" he adds, "not great, I had the most craziest dreams last night" Justin answers, although he is still not sure if he was dreaming or not as he pours himself a glass of orange juice, Justin walks down to the cellar, Justin figures that the cellar was so full of blood in his dream last night that if it really happened the blood would still be there, he gets down to the cellar and in to the room with the statue and much to his relief there is no blood anywhere, the place looks clean and tidy "thank God that was a dream Justin says to himself, he looks at the statue and like every other time he sees the statue Justin feels like it is watching him, he goes to walk out of the room as quick as he can but ends up walking in to one of the coffins, as he knocks the lid off his is horrified to see a pair of feet "oh shit" he says out loud, he looks up and sees its the body of John Jackson, again Justin attempts to run out of the room this time his dad is standing in the doorway "what did you do?" he cries, Justin holds his hands up "me, I did nothing" he shouts "you murdered three people" Justin adds, Dan looks at the dead bodies as they lay in there coffins "that was not me" Dan cries "something else taken control of me" he adds, they both look at the statue, "it's that ugly fuckin thing" Justin insists, Dan sits on the floor crying "what are we going to do" Justin looks at his dad crying, it's the first time he has ever seen his dad cry. Justin picks up a sledge hammer and smashes the statue with it, the hammer bounces off without even leaving a mark on it "I don't know what this statue is made of but the hammer does not touch it"

Justin tells his dad, Dan is still crying.

Chapter 14 Choices.

Justin attempts to smash the statue again, but again the sledge hammer does not even leave a mark on very solid statue, Justin is about to have another go when he hears a deep voice say "I wouldn't do that if I were you" he quickly turns his head and witnesses Dan standing there with huge black, dilated pupils "shit" Justin gasps, Dan starts walking towards Justin, Dan hisses at Justin "what are you?" Justin cries as he backs away, Dan's voice does not appear to be his own voice as he answers "I can be your worst nightmare or I can be your best friend," Justin is still backing away circling around a table with Dan stalking him, terrified that whatever has taken over his dads body might attack him Justin cries "what do you want?" Dan stops stalking Justin, he stands still "I am old and desperately weak, I have been trapped for nearly one hundred years" the deep voice that is coming from Dan's mouth explains, "what's this got to do with us?" Justin cries, Dan looks at Justin with eyes that horrify him "I take life from human beings, without them I am weak and I will die" the voice says "the three men that I received last night make me stronger but I will need more and I need you and your father to bring them to me" the deep demonic voice adds "no way" Justin says without even thinking "there can be no more murder" he adds, suddenly Justin loses consciousness he falls to the floor with a huge bang hitting his head on the wall as he falls, he has a very strange feeling as he stands up "what the fuck" he says to himself as the cellar looks different, the statue, the coffins, Dan and just about everything else in the room is gone, the cellar is completely empty, Justin is confused, he walks up the stairs when he comes to a door "who put the door there?" he thinks to himself.

He walks out of the cellar and in to the kitchen, the kitchen also looks different, when he walks in to the living room he sees his mom and Mandy sitting on the sofa, "your back" he says, neither of them react to him, Justin takes a closer look at them and sees that they are crying "what's wrong" he asks but again there is no reaction from them, Clare walks in to the room and sits on the chair, Justin runs up to her "Clare, Clare" he says right in front of her face, again there is no reaction, "what is going on?" Justin screams he notices Mandy looking at him and desperately runs up to her "Mandy" he says calmly, Mandy looks at Justin and then the television, Justin turns to see what she and everybody else in the room is so interested in, Sally turns the television up very loud Justin notices that both Sally and Clare are very interested in the news, the news reader begins to read the headlines at first Justin does not understand everybody's interest in the news then he hears his name mentioned "eighteen year old Justin Thomson is thought to have committed suicide by slitting his wrist in his prison cell due to the stress of his pending court trail that was due to start next week, Justin and his father the well known business man Daniel Thomson were accused of the ritualistic murders of three local men in Crudes castle" Justin turns around and looks at Mandy "no" he screams, Justin feels a huge drop in temperature, Justin looks around Mandy, Clare and Sally have gone but the television is still on, Justin looks at the TV and sees his dad sitting in the news readers seat, Justin takes a closer look, his eyes are still huge and his pupils are still dilated, he starts reading the news, Justin stares at the TV, "the news for you Justin is that I am your only hope, I can help you, I can allow you and your father to get away with the murders that you have committed in your cellar or I can expose you and your father as murderers and twisted Satanists, which will it be?" Justin screams "fuck you" at the very top of his voice when he opens his eyes he is back in the cellar, his dad his sitting on the floor, his eyes are now back to normal "what are we going to do?" Justin asks his dad "I don't think we have much choice other than to do what it says" his dad answers. They look at the statue as it stands perfectly still.

Dan vomits on the floor "we need to get rid of these dead bodies; they are starting to smell" he cries, "where are we going to put them?" Justin asks, suddenly they are interrupted by a loud bang, they both walk out from the room with the statue and in to the main room of the cellar, one of the huge sideboards is lying flat on the floor, Justin and Dan slowly walk over to investigate when they get there they see a hole in the wall, behind where the sideboard once stood they both grab a torch and go to investigate, Dan walks in first Justin closely follows him, there are a few cockroaches about and a huge dark tunnel, Justin and Dan slowly walk down the tunnel when they enter a huge underground cave like room, the room smells and looks more like the inside of a cave than a cellar and to their horror the room is full of bones and dead bodies "holy shit" Justin gasps as he looks around the dark cold room amazed at what he sees, "let's bring the bodies in here" Justin suggests, "I think that is what we are supposed to do" Dan replies. Dan and Justin decide to put the bodies in to the coffins and slide each coffin through between them. After an hour's hard work the bodies have been placed around the caved dark room with literally hundreds of other bodies and remains, most of the dead bodies appear to be at least one hundred years old some are just skeletons but Justin notices one of them looks fresh "dad" he shouts his dad walks over "look" Justin points at the body, Dan begins to investigate after looking at the body and some of the other bodies in the cellar, Dan quickly walks away "what's wrong?" Justin asks as his dad walks towards the way out "it looks like we are not the only ones hiding dead bodies in here" Dan says in a panic "come on let's get out of here" he says as Justin looks around the caved, dark, cold room he sees there are other ways to enter the room and he quickly follows his dad. When they get out of the tunnel they struggle to put the sideboard over the hole, after a huge struggle to move the very heavy sideboard they have finally covered the hole "what the fuck have we moved in to?" Justin asks as his dad is busy putting some of the objects back in to the very old sideboard hoping to make it as heavy and hard to move as he can for the fear that somebody else could enter his cellar through the hole.

Chapter 15. Back home

Its 1.00 pm by the time Dan and Justin have finished disposing of the bodies "whatever you do don't mention any of this to your mother" Dan tells Justin, Justin promises that he will not tell anyone "but what are we going to do about that statue?" he asks, Dan thinks about it for a few seconds and answers "I don't know yet, we will have to do as it says I guess" Justin is scared "we cannot keep killing people dad" he replies, Dan turns around "what choice do we have?" he moans "this thing could destroy our lives" he adds, Justin storms out of the living room. Later that day, just before 6.00 pm Sally, Clare, Jason and Mandy return, they all walk in to the house with their suit cases, Dan and Justin greet them, Sally looks around the house "no cockroaches to be seen anywhere" she happily says, Dan explains that there may be a couple around the house but the vast majority have been killed, Mandy walks around the living room "something feels different" she says to her mom, Justin and Dan both look at her "what feels different?" Dan asks, Mandy is holding her teddy bear "where is Mrs Morgan?" she asks, Sally rolls her eyes "I have already told you, she is dead" she angrily tells Mandy, Dan walks out of the room, two minutes later he walks back in to the room holding the stones he had brought from the old man "the cockroaches are not the only thing that we have managed to get rid off" Dan explains "these stones keep evil spirits like Mrs Morgan away" he adds, Mandy looks at the stones and drops her teddy bear on the floor "why did you get rid of Mrs Morgan?" she asks, "Mrs Morgan was helping us she is not an evil spirit" Mandy cries, Dan and Justin look at each other "how was she trying to help us?" Justin asks, Mandy picks her teddy bear up and walks out of the living room "I don't know" she mutters as she passes Justin and Dan "but she was" Mandy adds before walking upstairs and in to her bedroom, Sally looks at Dan "I don't know what is wrong with that child, but she keeps talking about Mrs Morgan" Sally explains, Dan shows Sally the stones "these should soon put a stop to that" he says, Sally picks one of the stones up and starts looking at it closely, "let's have a look down the cellar" she asks, Dan claims it is not safe and she must not enter it at all until he has had chance to have it looked "some of the ceiling looks like it's ready to drop" he explains.

Later that night Jason is playing his computer games, Mandy is sleeping, Clare is revising and Justin is searching the internet for stories about demons, the occult and his new home, Crudes Castle, the research is frightening him, first he discovers that Crudes castle has a history rich in human sacrifice, ritualistic murder, police cover ups and suicide, he also discovers that the robes he seen the people wearing at the standing stones while under the influence of LSD and in his cellar are robes used by an ancient secret society called the Ancient royal order of the red dragon, a secret society known for human sacrifice, murder, media manipulation and obviously secrecy, Justin reads and reads and the more he reads the more he is convinced that this "secret society" still exists, despite the official story that claims the secret society was destroyed in the year 1918.

Sally and Dan are down stairs watching TV when there is a knock at the door, Dan opens the door, its Detective Mark Green and his work colleague Constable George Jones, "can I help you?" Dan asks when Sally notices that it is the police she quickly walks to the front door, Detective Mark Green explains that he is looking for John Jackson, Anthony Collins and Jack Gould "they were last seen outside the Red Dragon talking to you Mr Thomson" Dan thinks about it, "I spoke to them for five minutes outside the pub" he explains "but they left and walked up to the castle with a bag of booze" he adds, Detective Mark Green asks "what were you talking about?" Dan thinks again "they were asking me about possible job openings, I told them that I needed local staff" he answers Sally looks at Dan she knows he is lying, Constable George Jones hands Dan a card "if you remember anything or you wish to talk feel free to contact us" Dan takes the card and thanks him, the police leave Dan shuts the door and walks in to the living room "what is going on?" Sally asks Dan, "I know that you would not offer them low life losers a job" she adds, Dan looks at Sally and says "I was threatening them because I was pissed about what they did to Justin, but then they left, I don't know where they went after that" he explains, Sally looks at Dan in the eyes "I hope that you have not done anything stupid" she says "I have not done anything stupid" Dan promises, Sally then she goes to bed she is not sure if she should believe Dan's story.

Chapter 16. Bankrupt.

The next day Sally gets up at half past seven she is surprised to see that Dan is already up and working in his office, she walks in the office and asks him why he is up so early, Dan has papers all over his desk "we have a bit of a problem" Dan says anxiously, "what's wrong" Sally asks, Dan is looking through hundreds of files, letters and receipts "our biggest customer went bust last night!" Dan explains, "we are fucked, they owe us hundreds of thousands" he adds, "there must be something we can do about it?" Sally asks, Dan looks at the paperwork "I don't know I have to see my solicitor" Dan picks his phone up and calls his solicitor, Sally walks out of the office and starts cleaning house. After an half an hour phone conversation Dan quickly walks out the house without even saying goodbye, "what's with dad?" Clare asks as she walks in to the living room, Sally runs to the car "where are you going?" she shouts to Dan, "I have to see my solicitor and my financial adviser" he answers, he starts up the car and quickly drives off.

Clare is sitting on the sofa eating her breakfast cereal when Justin walks in to the room and turns on the TV, "where is dad?" Justin asks, "I dunno, but he left in a hurry" Clare answers, Justin picks up yesterday's newspaper and starts reading when he is interrupted by a local news report on John Jackson, Anthony Collins and Jack Gould, Clare looks up at the TV "oh my god" he gasps, the news report claims that the three men seem to have "vanished without a trace and the police no leads" Justin breathes a sigh of relief when he notices Clare looking at him "what have you done?" she asks, "what?" Justin answers "I have not done anything" he adds, Clare does not know if she believes him or not.

Later that afternoon after a long meeting with his solicitor and financial adviser Dan gets back home, he pulls up outside the house and sits in the car for five minutes looking at the house, he sees Sally walking to the car "what's wrong?" she asks, Dan looks stressed "we have lost everything" Dan cries "we cannot afford the mortgage to this place, we are broke" Dan sighs as he steps out of the car and quickly walks to the house, when he gets in Clare and Justin are watching TV, "I suppose that you have been watching this shit all day again?" he says as he walks to the kitchen, he opens the drinks cupboard and pours himself a huge shot of whiskey, Sally walks in to the kitchen "what is going on?" she asks, Dan begins to explain, he explains that his business taken a huge loan to build a new warehouses and offices, "we believed we were doing the right thing, after all we had just won a seven year contract with one of the biggest food distributers in Britain" Dan explains "eighteen months later they cut their orders, it taken our profit down but we were OK, yesterday two years on the day that the contract started they tell me they have gone in to administration!" Dan adds as he drinks his whiskey. He goes on to explain that the company still owe him hundreds of thousands but he does not believe that he will ever see the money "the directors are still driving about in their BMWs" he moans, "and Bob Martins is living it up in his country mansion, holiday homes and Rolls Royce's" he adds as he picks up the bottle of whiskey and walks in to his office.

A couple of weeks later and Dan does not know what he is going to do about his bills, he has cancelled his payment for the mortgage and with Christmas just three days away and Clare eighteenth birthday coming up Dan knows he is about to spend what little money he has left, he gives Sally one thousand pound to get the Christmas presents and four hundred for the food and drinks over Christmas, Dan has about ten thousand pound left, but he has no income at all and the last thing that Dan wants to do is ask his parents for money, Christmas and the new year come and go and Dan's finances are quickly getting worse, Dan decides he must find a decent well paid job, only two days in to the new year and he is searching the internet for a job, he sends his C.V to many companies, he is starting to like the idea of doing something new and he is keen to get in to work, after days of looking and waiting for replies Dan is surprised that he still has not heard anything back from potential employers, Sally walks in to his office "when are you going to take the Christmas decorations down? she asks "I will do it now" Dan answers, "I am sick of seeing them anyway" he adds, After taking them down and putting them in to boxes Sally tells Dan to put them in the cellar, Dan starts walking down the stairs he puts the box down and goes to collect the other one, he walks back down the stairs, he puts the other box down and he is about to walk back up the stairs when he begins to have a short flash back of the night he murdered John, Ant and Jack, after the flashback he begins to slowly walk toward the room with the statue in it, he looks at the statue for a few seconds when he hears his wife's voice "I cannot stand that statue, it's so ugly" she says Dan looks at the statue and laughs.

Early hours at 3.03 am Dan is lying in bed sleeping when a voice wakes him, "come here, Dan, I can help you" the voice repeats two times Dan follows the sound of the voice, it seems to be coming from the cellar, Dan walks down to the cellar, to his surprise the statue is not standing in the room where it usually stands, its standing in the middle of the main part of the cellar, Dan hears the voice again "I can help you" the deep voice says, Dan looks up at the statue "How can you help me?" he asks, to Dan surprise the statue looks at him "give me your enemies and I will give you whatever you want" the statue claims, Dan was amazed to actually see the statue talking "you can have Bob Martin, the greedy bastard" Dan laughs, the statue smiles, the next thing Dan remembers is laying in bed and its 9.30 am he quickly gets out of bed "shit I slept in, I got to attend a job interview" he tells Sally as he runs out of the door, Dan gets to the interview late, he does not believe that the job interview went very well, he walks out of the new office blocks disappointed and desperate for money, he walks to a shop that he sees across the street he buys a bottle of wine and a scratch card and he gets back in to his car he is just about to scratch the ticket when a huge church across the street catches his eye, the building looks ancient with huge trees all around it and a cemetery in front of the church. Then a gargoyle very similar to the one he seen at the Coopers house and very similar to the one in his cellar only smaller catches his eye, he tries to take a closer look when he is distracted by a traffic warden "I'm going" Dan shouts as the traffic warden is about to give him a ticket, the traffic warden walks away, Dan looks up at the church only to see that the Gargoyle is gone! Dan scratches the scratch card that he bought from the shop minutes earlier and to his utter amazement and delight he discovers that his card has won fifty thousand pounds, "yes" Dan shouts at the top of his voice "fuckin yes" he shouts again passionately, he looks at the scratch again just to make sure and again he celebrates. At dinner time Dan arrives home with a huge smile on his face, Sally opens the door "what are you laughing at" she asks him "did you get the job" Dan smiles "I done better then that" he happily says, he hands his wife the scratch card, his wife looks at it and cheers "It is not enough" Dan claims "but it's not a bad start" he adds, Sally cannot believe it as she keeps checking the scratch card just to make sure.

Later that night all the children are in bed except for Justin, Justin is at the pub with his friend Carl Cooper, Clare is watching TV in bed and the younger two are sleeping, Sally and Dan are sitting on the sofa talking about what they are going to do with their money "we have to invest it wisely, in to setting up a small business" Dan insists "maybe a small shop of some description" he adds, when suddenly a news report interests them, the new reader reads "Bob Martin was a successful business man until last week when his food distributing company went in to administration costing over seven hundred people their jobs, since then Bob Martin was heavily criticized by his former staff and the local media for cashing in on the misfortune of his former staff" Dan looks at Sally, they then both look back at the television, the news reader continues "police have confirmed that the decapitated body found at his huge mansion in Kent was Bob Martin, police have also confirmed that they are yet to find his head" Dan turns off the television and sits down "shit" he gasps, Sally sips her wine "well if you rip off hundreds of people you should expect at least one of them to come after you" Dan is shocked and horrified, he thinks of the dream that he had in the early hours of the morning, he remembers saying "you can have Bob Martin, the greedy bastard" Dan thinks about the scratch card win, Sally is still talking about Bob Martin's death, Dan just stands up and says "I'm going to bed" Sally watches as Dan walks out of the living room and up the stairs, she thinks that something she said might have upset Dan.

The next day and Dan seems in a better mood, Mandy and Jason are eating their breakfast and Clare and Justin are still in bed, Sally explains to Dan that she is going to visit her friend "I am taking Jason and Mandy" she adds, Dan tells Sally that he "is going to clean the cellar out today, now we know it is safe" Sally tells the children to "hurry and eat their breakfast" as she picks up her bag and begins to search it for the car keys, after ten minutes Sally, Mandy and Jason leave, Dan walks down to the cellar.

Chapter 17.Vivid vision.

As Dan enters the cellar he is stunned to see that the statue is standing in the middle of the main part of the cellar instead of the room he had last seen it in, then he remembers his dream, "what the fuck are you" Dan gasps, then he notices a very old looking book in front of the statue, Dan slowly walks up to the book and picks it up. The book has a leather cover and is written in red and although the book is written in Latin it does not take Dan long to see that the statue that he has in his cellar is mentioned in the book and art that contains strange looking creatures is also featured, some of the art shows creatures that are almost identical in appearance to the statue that Dan is looking at. Dan looks at the statue intensely "did you kill Bob Martin" he asks, the statue stands still, Dan gets a little more angry "what the fuck are you" he shouts, "why don't you leave me the fuck alone" he adds, when he is interrupted by Clare "what are you doing?" she asks, Dan quickly thinks of a lie "there is something flying about in here" he answers, Clare looks around but does not see anything then she looks at the statue "whatever" she sighs and she walks up the stairs, Dan looks at the statue and follows Clare up the stairs. Justin is in the kitchen eating his breakfast "what are you doing in the cellar" he asks his dad as his dad enters the kitchen, Dan looks at Clare and then back at Justin "I was setting some more traps for the cockroaches, I think there could be a Bat or something down there" he answers.

After twenty minutes Justin and Clare leave the house Dan walks back down to the cellar, the statue is still in the middle of the cellar this time there is a wooden box in front of the statue, Dan slowly walks up to the statue, he notices a puddle of blood under the box, "what the fuck" he gasps he slowly takes the lid of the box and looks inside only to see Bob Martin's head looking back at him "fuck" he shouts as he drops the box on the floor, Bob Martin's head rolls out of the box, his face is frozen, he has an expression of panic and fear, Dan screams and tries to run, but he slips and falls over hitting his head on the hard blood covered floor.

Dan quickly stands up "what are you?" Dan asks looking at the statue, Dan is sure that the statue is smiling at him, he feels like he is going crazy, then to his amazement Bob Martin walks out from behind the statue "thank you" for the gift, Bob Martin says, Dan is stunned, he just stands still for a few seconds with his mouth wide open "what is going on" he asks, Bob Martin walks up to the kitchen and pours himself a huge shot of Dan's whiskey, Dan follows him and watches in amazement "you are supposed to be dead" Dan tells him, Bob turns his head towards Dan, has a huge sip of whiskey and begins to explain "Bob Martin is dead, I am what you would call a spirit, a spirit trapped in a dark, dead lonely world for nearly one hundred years until you freed me, thank you for that by the way" he smiles at Dan, Dan looks bewildered, Bob Martin carries on talking "I need your help, after all I helped you are you enjoying your fifty thousand pound win?" Dan remembers the Gargoyle at the church that seemed to be watching him, Bob Martin carries on "I need you to bring me the body of a young male of perfect innocence, he must be alive for me to perform the ritual on" Dan interrupts "what for?" he asks, Bob smiles again "this body is useless to me, he is already about sixty years old, I want a fresh one" Dan backs away "no fucking way" he cries, "I cannot do that" he adds, Bob's eyes turn black and his face looks angry "you will do it because I need you to do it" he shouts in Dan's face, Dan has an idea "use the bodies of John, Jack and Ant" Bob explains that their energies were used "on allowing his spirit to cross back in to our world" Dan refuses again "no way am I bringing anyone to you" he shouts when Bob grabs his arm, Dan begins to have a vivid vision.

In this vivid, nightmarish vision he is in a prison cell but he is not alone, he sees a figure in the cell with him, Dan just looks around for a few seconds wondering where he is and what is going on, then he notices that the other person in the cell is crying, he recognizes the sound of the crying "Justin" Dan whispers, there is no reply from Justin, he simply carries on crying "Justin" Dan whispers again, again Justin does not respond, Justin then puts his hand to his feet as if he is looking for something, to Dan's horror he pulls out a Stanley blade out of his sock, "Justin" Dan shouts "what are you going to do with that" he shouts louder still, Justin holds it to his wrist and bursts in to tears, Dan quickly run towards to stop him but he cannot feel or touch him, it's like he is a hologram. Justin digs the blade in to his left wrist and cuts it upwards, then he does his right wrist "help" Dan shouts "help" then a figure catches his eye, its Bob Martin "you know, it does not have to be like this" he says calmly as Justin is bleeding to death in front of them "I can stop this, I can give you anything you want, all I want is a body, if you help me I can help you" Justin dies, Dan watches as his spirit leaves his body and a bright light shines in front of them, Justin's spirit looks at Dan for a couple of seconds, then he looks at the bright light and begins to walk towards the light, but then Dan notices the light gets less bright, it gets dimmer and dimmer by the second and then turns black, Dan sees demons and devils coming for Justin, "what do they want" he asks, Bob Martin smiles again "his soul" he answers "no" Dan screams as he watches strange evil looking creatures stalking his son's spirit, then he looks around, he is back in his cellar and Bob Martin is nowhere to be seen. Dan looks around the cellar for five minutes he is confused, scared and he cannot get the thought of Justin's suicide out of his head, he goes upstairs.

He falls on the sofa he feels exhausted and sick he just sits there thinking, he thinks about his visions, he thinks about Justin's face as he slit his own wrists, he pictures a face of sadness, desperation and despair "I cannot let that happen" Dan says to himself "I will not let this happen" he adds, he paces up and down the living room thinking about what he should do, he quickly runs back down to the cellar and stands in front of the statue "I will bring you a young male" he sighs, just please do not let Justin go to prison, Dan looks at the statue waiting for some kind of sign but the statue remains perfectly still "give me a sign" Dan screams then he hears his wife's voice "what are you doing?" she asks, Dan runs up to her and says "listen you have to stay at my parents house for a couple of nights" Sally shakes her head "no way" she answers "why?" she asks, Dan quickly thinks of another lie "I have just found more cockroaches and I need to put poison down, it may not be very safe for the kids" Sally looks around the cellar she does not see any cockroaches "I don't care" she says, "I would rather be around cockroaches then your mother" she adds, Dan looks at her "what's that supposed to mean?" he asks, then Sally's mobile phone begins to ring Sally answers the phone and walks out of the cellar leaving Dan in the cellar, Dan walks up the stairs, he walks in to the bathroom, when he sees Bob Martin in the mirror, he quickly turns around expecting to see Bob Martin behind him, but Bob Martin is not there, he looks back at the mirror only to see Bob Martin standing there looking back at him "you got two days to bring me a young male" a voice that sounds like it is coming from behind him says, "two days" Dan complains, Bob Martin's reflection disappears, Dan quickly walks out of the bathroom, he hears Sally crying "what's wrong?" he asks "it is my mom" Sally answers "she had an heart attack last night" she cries, "I have to go and see her" she adds, Sally takes Jason and Mandy with her as she rushes to an hospital the other side of the country.

Later that night Dan starts planning on how he will kidnap an eighteen to twenty year old male when Justin walks in to the house "where's mom?" he asks, Dan explains that Justin's grandmother has been rushed to hospital after an heart attack, Clare walks in to the room "I am going to bed" she says and she walks upstairs, Justin starts telling his dad about the long list of occult killings that have gone on in this area "look at this" Justin excitedly says as he hands his dad an envelope full of papers, "I went to the city archives the other day" Justin explains " I found at least forty different stories of ritualistic murders in this area, dating back from 1789" he adds, Dan looks at the newspaper prints and says "I have not got time to look at this bullshit" and then he walks in to the kitchen a pours himself a drink, Justin picks up the newspaper prints "whatever" he mutters as he walks to his bedroom.

Chapter 18 Kidnap

The next day comes and Dan gets up early and continues to try and make a plan on his kidnapping, he uses the internet in order to see how people have been caught and how people have got away with it in the past, armed with chloroform that he found in the cellar, Dan puts sunglasses and a hat on and walks out of his house and in to his car, he starts the car up and drives to the local school, he parks outside and looks in his mirror only to see Bob Martins face looking back at him, Dan notices that he looks weaker than he did yesterday weaker and older, Dan also senses a bit of desperation from the creature that inhabits Bob Martin's body "how will I know if he is of perfect innocence?" Dan asks, he sits there for five minutes before a young male aged seventeen walks past, Dan looks in the mirror "this one will do" the creature says, pointing at the young man "get him now" he adds, Dan sits there "I can't do it" he cries, the creature frowns angrily, "need I remind you what's at stake" Bob Martin mutters, Dan bursts in to tears "I can't do it" he cries again, Dan looks in the mirror only to see that Bob's face has gone, Dan is not sure what to call the creature so he shouts "Bob" there is no answer, he seems to have completely disappeared, Dan looks around the car and then back in to the mirror, this time he does not see Bob Martins, this time he sees the desperate, scared look on Justin's face just before the suicide that Dan witnessed in his nightmarish vision, Dan screams "no" and when he looks again he sees his own reflection "fuck you" Dan screams "fuck you" he screams again, he punches the mirror in his car smashing it to pieces and cutting his hand open at the same time, than Dan hears a knocking sound, he looks outside his car only to see two policemen, Dan opens his window, "can I help you" he asks one of the policemen, the police puts his head in to the car looks around and says "we have had reports from locals that you have been parked outside here for over an hour and half talking to yourself" Dan thinks quick "I was on the phone" he tells the police "I was using my hands free" he adds, Dan shows the policeman his hands free, the policemen look at each other and then at Dan, one puts his head in the car "are you going to move on now?" he asks "yes" Dan answers nervously, the police officers walk back to their car. There was a big sigh of relief from Dan once the policemen had gone, he starts the car and drives off.

Dan is only driving for a minute before he notices somebody sitting next to him, he jumps back with a fright as he turns his head he discovers that Bob Martin is sitting next to him, he loses control of the car for just a second, he nearly drives off the road "can you like stop doing that shit" he screams at Bob, Bob sits next to Dan smiling "where are you going?" Bob asks Dan, "home" Dan answers "forget it, you want a body, you get a body" Dan adds, Bob smiles and vanishes Dan drives home and lays on the sofa when he hears movement upstairs, he slowly walks up the stairs when he hears more movement coming from Clare's room, Dan walks in to the room, Clare is in the room with her twenty year old male friend, they are kissing as Dan walks in "what the fuck do you think you are doing?" he asks Clare, Clare jumps out of her skin "dad" she gasps "this is James he is my studying partner" she adds, Dan smiles and walks down the stairs. James looks at Clare, Clare is confused by her dad's actions she quietly tells James to leave the house James argues for a couple of seconds "I will see you Tuesday" Clare tells him, James gives her a kiss walks downstairs he is about to leave the house when Dan calls James in to the kitchen.

James has a quick look to see if Clare is coming down the stairs, he then slowly walks in to the kitchen "so you are James, my daughter's boyfriend" he says, "what do you like about her?" Dan asks, James thinks about what he is going to say very carefully, then he answers "I like her personality, she is nice" Dan laugh's "I bet you fuckin do son" he jokes, James smiles but inside he feels very uncomfortable and nervous. Dan offers James a glass of whiskey at first James refuses insisting that he does not drink, Dan messes around and calls James "a woman and a pussy" eventually and inevitably James takes the glass and has a sip, after one sip James is coughing and heaving, Dan smiles as he puts a bottle of Lysergic acid diethylamide in his pocket after putting a huge dose in James's drink.

Clare is sitting in her bedroom listening to music when suddenly the track she is listening to comes to an end, she hears bad coughing and rushes down the stairs "dad" she shouts as she bursts in to the living room Clare is surprised to see that James is still there "James" she gasps "what are you still doing here?" she asks, James is about is explain when Dan interrupts "he is having a drink with me" Dan explains, James is sitting in the living room and he feels very strange,

Clare looks at James "are you drunk?" she asks "no" James answers "I only had a tiny shot" he adds, Dan laughs "yeah and you acted like a bitch drinking that" Clare is shocked "come on James you should go now" she says "nonsense" Dan shouts as he pours them both a drink, Clare is confused by her dads actions and when Justin walks into the house Clare is happy to him "dad is pissing me off" Clare moans to Justin "he has got James drunk now he has to walk home in this state" she adds Justin looks at James, James seems relaxed and happy "he does not seem to mind" Justin says Clare rolls her eyes in despair. Justin and Clare walk in to the living room Justin sits on the chair, Dan notices a dark hooded figure stalking Justin, the figure looks at Dan with its demonic face and smiles then it disappears, Clare sits next to James on the sofa "so how long have you two known each other" Dan asks "about three months" James answers "Clare and I were in the same art classes" he adds "how old are you?" Dan asks "twenty" James replies, Dan rubs his hands together he hears a voice in his head "this is your chance" the voice mutters. Dan asks many more questions, he asks about James's family, his childhood and his job and ambitions, Clare notices that the questions are getting more personal and James feels more and more nervous "are you a virgin?" Dan asks, Clare puts her head in her hands feeling huge embarrassment, James also feels embarrassed "yes" James answers, Dan grins "good" he mutters, Clare storms off upstairs, Justin looks at Dan "what are you doing?" he asks, "I am saving your life and your soul" Dan answers, "tell Clare that James is going home now" he orders Justin "I will show him to the door" Dan adds. Justin walks upstairs and in to Clare's bedroom "he has gone home now" Justin tells Clare "I am going to bed" Clare replies Justin walks in to his bedroom and turns on his TV.

Chapter 19. Good Dan vs Evil Dan.

Dan led's James in to his cellar, James is starting to have mild hallucinations "what was that?" he asks, Dan looks around "there is nothing there" he answers, Dan looks at James, he look nervous and jumpy "what the fuck is wrong with you?" Dan asks, James is looking around the cellar "nothing, I'm fine" he answers, then James looks up at the statue "what is that?" he asks as he looks at the statue intensely, there is no answer from Dan, James takes his eyes off the statue and looks at Dan, Dan looks worried "get out of here quick" he cries, James looks around "why?" he asks, "follow me" Dan says as he sneaks towards the exit, the lights turn off for a few seconds leaving them in pitch black darkness "shit" Dan cries after about forty five seconds the lights turn back on. James looks up at Dan only to see two versions of Dan looking at each other, one version of Dan looks angry and almost demonic the other version looks worried, scared and he is backing away "let James go" the scared version of Dan says as he continues to back away from the angry version "fuck him, give him to the spirits, they will help you, reward you and save your son" the angry version snarls. James does not know what is real and what is not he feels confused, paranoid and very scared he is about to run towards the exit but as he looks up to work out the quickest possible escape route he discovers that he is surrounded by a circle of hooded men, James cannot see their faces but the chanting noise is making his hair stand up.

James looks around him to only to see that there are eight hooded men and the huge statue, the hooded men have made a circle of bodies surrounding what James perceives to be evil Dan and nice Dan and himself, the statue is also a part of the circle James sees no escape, he screams and screams but nobody hears, he falls to the ground and looks at the nice version of Dan, Dan looks back, Dan is just about to say something when a demonic, snake eyed version of Dan attacks him. Dan tries to defend himself but the evil version seems stronger and he throws Dan around, James notices that the evil version of Dan has huge black eyes the sight of him terrifies James as he cries "what the fuck is going on" he watches as the friendly version of Dan is fighting for his life, a hooded man gives both of the Dan's a sword each and orders them to fight, Dan gets ready to defend himself but Dan with the dilated pupils is a lot aggressive, good Dan looks scared, worried and he is fighting just to survive, evil Dan swings his sword around recklessly trying to kill good Dan but good Dan keeps his distance and dodges the swinging sword. After three minutes of sword fighting evil Dan throws his sword over the hooded figures and runs towards good Dan, knocking him to the ground and holding him down, evil Dan then bites good Dan on the face taking off a chunk of his cheek and chewing it, he spits it at James "he is chewing his fuckin face off" he laughs James nearly vomits, good Dan smashes evil Dan in the face with his fist, the punch seems to have an effect on evil Dan and good Dan holds him down and lands seven more hard punches all to the face leaving evil Dan face down on the floor in a puddle on his own blood. Good Dan stands up and tries to catch his breath "now let me go" he shouts, the hooded men do not move, James stands up and looks at Dan, he sees a figure slowly creeping up on Dan, James looks at where evil Dan was laying only to discover that he had gone leaving a bloody puddle and a trail of blood, before James even gets chance to shout "watch out" evil Dan swings his sword cutting his good counterparts head off, James screams in absolute fear Dan walks up to him "now we are ready for you" he says, Bob Martin walks out from behind the statue.

Bob looks at James and then looks at Dan "he is a bit of a lame little fucker" he says, Dan looks at James "yeah he is" he answers "but he is all I could get" Bob looks at James again "he will have to do I suppose" he moans, James sees Bob's face changing, he believes he sees a demon inside him, Bob stands in the middle of the circle, the hooded figures start chanting louder, two hooded men hold James still, James sees the face of one of the men, the face is horrifying he screams at the top of his voice and tries to escape, Justin hears the screaming as he opens the door Clare is also standing outside of her bedroom "what is dad doing?" she asks "I will go and check" Justin answers, he begins to slowly walk down the stairs. The hooded men place James in the middle of the circle James notices there are strange symbols painted on the floor, Bob Martin walks up to James, Bob is holding a syringe he injects James with a lethal dose of Barbiturate, the chanting continues, James feels drowsy and weak, he looks at the head of good Dan and notices the head apart from its body is crying "I'm sorry" Dan's head shouts, evil Dan walks up to the head and stamps on it, Dan's severed head screams in pain evil Dan laughs and James slowly dies, Dan walks up to the body of James to check for life "he's dead" he says Bob Martin smiles. Two of the hooded men hold the body of James up they then continue with the chanting.

Dan watches as one of the hooded men step in to the middle of the circle, Bob Martin falls to his knees "I am ready" he calmly says, the huge hooded figure picks up a huge sword covered with strange symbolism and he slits the throat of Bob Martin, Bob Martin falls to the ground as his blood covers the floor, one of the hooded men places a chair in to the middle of the circle, the two hooded men holding up James's dead body place James in to the chair, Dan watches with huge interest as the hooded figures are still chanting, Justin is standing by the stairs in his cellar, he wants to investigate what is going on in the cellar but he feels panic and fear like never before, he recognizes the chanting from his hallucinations and dreams, Justin slowly walks down the stairs and in to the main room of the cellar when he enters the cellar the chanting comes to an abrupt end, Justin is surprised to see Dan and James's lifeless body sitting on the chair. "What the fuck have you done to him?" Justin gasps at Dan, Dan looks at the dead body "it wasn't me" he cries, Justin slowly walks towards James, James is perfectly still until Justin notices his finger twitching "what happened to him" Justin shouts at Dan when Clare interrupts "what happened to who?" she asks dreading the answer, she sees James sitting on the chair, to Dan's surprise James stands up "I am fine" he says as he walks up to Clare and kisses her on the cheek, Clare looks at Dan, Dan is confused "well Daniel it's been nice talking to you and I expect I will see you soon" James says, Dan feels intimidated he knows that it is not James in that body, James is walking out of the Thomson's garden when Dan shouts him back "who are you?" Dan asks, James smiles and answers "from this day onward my name is James Cohens, I am going to my new home with my new mom and dad" James walks away slowly.

Dan walks in to the kitchen when Clare asks him "what were you and James talking about?" Dan pours himself a glass whiskey and says "nothing much, I am going to bed now" and he walks out of the kitchen, Clare looks at Justin "he is so embarrassing" she moans, Justin laughs.

The next day comes Justin and Clare are downstairs eating their breakfast, Dan is still in bed, "dad" Clare shouts up the stairs, there is no reply, Clare walks up the stairs and in to his bedroom, Dan is in a deep sleep and Clare decides not to wake him, she walks out of the house and makes her way to college, Justin turns the TV on and sits down to watch it meanwhile Dan is dreaming, he is wondering around lost in pitch black darkness, he feels scared to move because his cannot see the floor, he feels with his hands but there is nothing around him until he sees a small light in the distance "help" Dan shouts but nobody can hear him, Dan desperately tries to walk towards the light until he hears a growling noise, he stands as still as he can, he looks at the light again and slowly starts to walk towards it but the light vanishes and Dan wakes up, he gets out of bed and gets himself ready he knows that Sally could be back home today.

Its 7.00 pm before Sally, Mandy and Jason get home, they walk in to the house, Dan does not appear to be there, Sally hears movement in the cellar she looks at the kids and she orders them "to watch T.V for ten minutes when I do you some food" the children turn on the T.V, Sally walks down the cellar to discover Dan cleaning the statue "why are you cleaning that horrible thing?" Sally asks, Dan is angered by

Sally's remarks but he hides it as well as he can "because it was dirty" Dan calmly answers, he walks past Sally and upstairs Sally follows him "what's wrong with you?" she asks him "nothing" he answers as he walks in to the living room where Mandy and Jason are watching television, Mandy looks at him and runs to her mom, Jason gives him a hug "alright pal" Dan says to Mandy, Mandy holds on to her mother, Sally pushes her away and says "stop being silly" Dan looks shocked by her reaction to him he kneels down "ain't you going to give your daddy a kiss?" Dan says "you are not my daddy" Mandy angrily answers, Dan stands up and walks in to the kitchen, Sally follows him "take no notice of her, she is very tired it's been a long journey" she says, Dan smiles and gives Sally a hug, as he is hugging her he looks over her shoulders at Mandy, Mandy is looking back at him, he smiles at her, she looks the other way. Not long after Justin and Clare walk in to the house and ask Sally "where is dad?" "he is in his office, I think" Sally answers, Justin explains that Dan has been acting very strange, Sally dismisses it "maybe he is a bit stressed" she says before walking in to his office and asking him if he would like a coffee.

A couple of days later and Dan is more like his usually self, but inside he still feels confused and upset about what he has done, Dan is watching Mandy as she plays in the garden, Mandy looks at him and waves, Dan smiles and waves back, Dan looks up and sees Clare holding hands with James, he watches and gets angry, Clare kisses him and walks down the drive, James gets in to his car and drives off, Dan watches Clare as she goes to walk in to the house "Clare" he shouts she looks around and sees him, she walks to the entrance to the back garden, she notices he looks angry and she guesses that he saw her kissing James "you cannot see that kid anymore" Dan orders, Clare sighs "dad I am eighteen, you cannot tell me who I can and cannot see" she angrily replies, "you don't understand" Dan says, "he is not who you think he is" he adds, Clare walks off ignoring her dads request.

Chapter 20. Murder.

Weeks go by and Dan does not hear nothing from James, until one day in April, when Dan is driving back from the supermarket, he is stuck in what first appears to be a traffic jam after twenty minutes of not moving Dan is getting frustrated "fucking police" he moans "they close these roads for nothing" he adds. After five more minutes the traffic finally moves allowing Dan to move about forty yards. Dan and Sally notice that there are six police cars and two ambulances parked outside a huge house, the house is surrounded by trees and fields, Dan notices that even the news channels are there, "I wonder what has happened here?" Sally says Dan is looking around when he notices James Cohens standing in the front garden of the house using his phone. James looks up and sees Dan looking at him, he smiles and waves Dan quickly drives off without paying attention to where he is going he nearly runs in to a elderly woman crossing the road "watch out" Sally screams, Dan apologizes to her and drives past the traffic on the wrong side of the road “what are you doing?” Sally cries “I just want to get back home as quick as I can” Dan answers.

Dan gets in to his house and quickly turns on the news at but there is no mention of anything, he goes on the internet and by using social networking sites he discovers that Terry and Cassandra Cohens (James Cohen parents) were discovered dead at 2.30 this afternoon, Dan looks at his watch, it’s now 6.00pm, the post was by a neighbour and according to the internet post; police have not released anymore information yet but Dan has a bad feeling. Later that night Dan and Sally have planned to go to the local pub for a drink, Dan tells Clare and Justin to make sure they "watch the kids" they then walk out of the house and make their way to the pub.

The next day comes and Dan gets out of bed later than usual when he gets downstairs he is shocked to see James is in his living room talking to Sally and Clare, James looks upset and Clare is holding his hand, Sally walks up to Dan and whispers "it's terrible what that poor kid has gone through" Dan looks over at Clare and James "what’s happened?" Dan asks, Sally explains how James found his parents and his uncle dead, "massacred, a bloody mess according to James, heads cut off and the killer or killers have not been found" she goes on to explain how police suspect the murder is linked to "some kind of underground network of Satanists" Dan already has his own suspicions, "it must be terrible for the poor kid, I mean image finding your parents like that" she adds before Dan interrupts "listen, I got to go somewhere, do not leave Clare alone with him" Dan orders, he runs to his car and drives off.

When Dan leaves his drive he is surprised to see Detective Mark

Green and Constable George Jones sitting in their car outside of Dan's front Garden, Dan drives his cars close to theirs and opens his window, Detective Mark Green opens his window as well "can I help you officers?" Dan asks "we did actually want to asks you a few questions" Detective Mark Green answers, Dan rolls his eyes "go on then" Dan says, Detective Mark Green asks Dan if he would like to talk somewhere "more private" Dan declines "no here is fine with me" he answers, Constable George Jones takes a note pad and gets ready to write "where were you at between 1.30 pm and 3.00 pm yesterday" the Detective asks, Dan laughs "what, you think I killed the Cohens?" Dan asks, Detective Mark Green remains straight faced "just answer the question please" he orders, "I was with my wife in the supermarket and then I was sat in the traffic caused by the police blocking the whole street for over an hour and half" Dan answers sharply "Don't believe me? my wife is in the house now ask her" he adds, Dan starts his car up "is there anything else I can help you with?" he asks with a hint of sarcasm "that's all for now" Detective Mark Green answers, Dan speeds off, "since that family have moved in to this area three people have gone missing they were last seen talking to Daniel Thomson, one person has committed suicide in Dan Thomson's house and now three people have been brutally murdered" Detective Mark Green says, they get out of the car and walk to Dan's house. The police officers are surprised to see James Cohens at the Thomson's house, they take Sally in to a different room and ask Sally if she can confirm her husband's story to which she answers "yes, of course, you don't think my husband could have killed the Cohens, do you?" she asks the police officers leave the house with very few leads to follow.

Dan drives to the Cohens huge mansion, he sees that there are three police cars parked outside the house as police and forensics are still looking for evidence, Dan gets out of his car and walks up to the house, Dan puts his face up to the window to get a look at what might of happened, he sees the room is still covered in blood but he also notices symbols drawn all over the walls and floor, Dan notices the symbols are very similar or maybe even the same as the symbols that were used at the rituals he had taken part of. Dan quickly runs back to his car, he begins to drive, he has the idea of going back to the Little shop of Magik, he drives to town parks his car and begins walking to the shop, he passes all the shops and remembers his way there with ease yet when he gets there he is shocked and confused to discover that there is no Little shop of Magik there, it's an empty until, he walks up to the window of the unit and looks through it, the window is dusty and the unit appears to have been empty for a long time, Dan steps away from the unit and looks around to make sure he is in the right place, when he looks around him he notices an old building, the building is placed in the middle of the high street and it is now used as a office units, Dan notices the building is full of strange symbolism and even gargoyles, then he notices one of the gargoyles appear to be looking right at him, he looks back at the unit where he expected to see the Little shop of Magik and starts to quickly walk to his car. He gets to his car gets in and drives home quickly, it takes him fifteen minutes to get home when he gets to the house he bursts through the door and walks in to the living room, he grabs the black stones that he brought from the Little shop of Magik, he walks up to the top of his back garden and throws them in to a stream, when he walks back down the garden he sees Mandy watching him through her bedroom window she smiles and waves at him Dan waves back.

Dan walks in to his house and in the living room where Justin is watching T.V "where is Clare?" Dan asks Justin, Justin does not answer he has earphones in listening to music, Dan taps his shoulder and Justin takes the earphones out "what?" Justin says, "Where is Clare?" Dan asks again, "I don't know" Justin answers "last time I seen her she was with James" he adds, Dan stands up and starts getting angry "I told her to stay away from him" he moans, Justin rolls his eyes "give the guy a break dad, his whole family have just been murdered" Justin cries, "and anyway I would be nice to James he is the sole beneficiary of the family fortune which apparently is fucking huge," Justin adds, "what family fortune?" Dan asks, Justin explains that James's family are "part of the aristocracy with royal connections, hundreds of businesses and millions of pounds and I have not even mentioned the thirty bedroom mansion" Dan is horrified by this news "James killed them" Dan tells Justin. Justin is shocked by what his dad has just told him "why would James kill his own parents?" Justin asks, "there was a ritual, I was there but I cannot remember it very well, it was like a dream but I know it was real" Dan says, Justin starts to listen with interest "that thing that is in James's body is not James Cohens, it's some kind of spirit or curse that was in that statue" Dan says, at first Justin finds it hard to believe his dad, he thinks his dad might be losing his mind, but then Justin remembers some of the news articles on ritualistic murders in Crudes Castle, he remembers seeing James sitting lifeless in the chair and he remembers the rituals he has seen in his dreams and his hallucinations, Justin begins to believe what Dan is telling him, he then remembers a photo dated July 1919, he goes to the cupboard that the old newspapers and photographs from the cellar were put and shows Dan a photograph, the A4 photo shows Henry Cohens and Charles Cooper standing by a Rolls Royce Phianna Limo, behind them he sees part of Crudes Castle and three trees, "what's this got to do with anything?" Dan asks, "Look at the back" Justin says Dan sees the names Henry Cohens and Charles Cooper and the date July 1919, "that is the wrong date" Dan points outs "Justin looks at the photograph and asks "how do you know that?" Dan takes the photograph back "if this photograph was taken in July the trees would be full of leaves and there would be flowers or weeds growing on the edge of the road" he explain "oh my God you are right" Justin gasps.

Later that night Clare walks in alone, its 10.30 pm and Dan is annoyed that she has not been in touch "where have you been?" Dan asks his daughter, "with James" Clare answers "he is so upset" she adds, "yeah right" Dan quietly mutters to himself, "I don't want you hanging around him" Dan tells Clare "he is a nasty piece of work" he adds, Clare storms out of the living room, she walks upstairs, Sally playing a board game with Jason and Mandy so Dan sneaks down to the cellar. Upon entering the cellar Dan sees that the statue is not in the main part of the cellar anymore, it's in the room that Dan first found it in, Dan walks in to the room and is horrified to see three severed heads on the statue in front of him, they are the heads of the Cohens, then Dan hears a cough he quickly turns around to discover James in his cellar "what are you doing in my house" Dan asks sharply, James smiles "I was here a long time before you and I will still be here a long time after you are gone" he snarls at Dan "what do you want now?" Dan asks, "I am looking for a bride, I am young, rich, well educated and I have great prospects for the future, would you give me your blessing to marry your daughter, Clare Thomson" Dan is shocked and angered by the question, he runs up to James and begins to punch him "keep away from my fucking family" Dan shouts, Dan grabs James and he is ready to inflict some punishment when Dan suddenly feels paralyzed, "you will give your blessing, if you do not I will kill her" James says, he then vanishes without a trace, Dan can now move again.

Dan has no idea what he can do to stop his daughter marrying James, he puts the heads in to bags on carries them through to the caves that are joined on to his cellar, when Dan is walking through with the severed heads when he becomes aware that somebody else has been in the caved room, he sees at least six fresh bodies and wonders how they could have got there, then Dan sees a different exit, he decides to walks through a tunnel, after ten minutes of walking he sees light at the end of the tunnel, he walks to the light and comes out by the standing stones at the back of the castle, Dan notices a group of hooded men in the distance, "shit" he says quietly to himself, he quickly walks back home.

Meanwhile Justin is searching local history of Crudes Castle on the internet, after only ten minutes of searching he finds a lot of interesting information on Henry Cohens, he discovers that Henry Cohens was murdered by two local men namely James Green and Charles Cooper he also discovers a local website claiming that Henry Cohens was possessed by the devil, the website claims he was killed to protect

Crudes Castle and the local people but he pledged he would return. Old newspaper reports show that a huge amount of ritualistic murders were taking place in Crudes Castle at the time and many locals believed that Henry Cohens had something to do with them, then Justin starts looking at historic pictures of Crudes Castle, he gets a few pictures taken from the early nineteen hundreds then he comes to August 1917 he notices that there is a picture of James Green and Charles Cooper with a group of suited men, he flicks past a few pictures before come to a picture taken in July 1919, it's a picture of the standing stones but Justin notices something strange about the picture, its July yet the trees have no leaves, they are bare as if it is the middle of December like the picture he and his dad found in the cellar. Justin searches Crudes Castle 1919 to look at a few more pictures, he notices that pictures taken in July and August 1919 all show that there were no leaves on the trees at that time, he looks at pictures from the summer of 1920 and discovers the same yet in the summer of 1921 the trees appears to have leaves on them, not as many as they should but by 1922 the tress were fully blooming, Justin rushes down stairs to show Dan what he has found by now Dan is falling asleep in front of the television, Justin shows Dan, though Dan is interested he does not know what to make of it "its weird alright" Dan says, "but what does it mean?" he asks, "I don't know" Justin answers.

Chapter 21. Ritual.

A few months go by and the Thomson's do not hear anything of James, it was just business as usual in Crudes Castle, its April but the weather has been cold for the time of year, Dan is running out of money again due to a couple of bad investments and having to pay the high mortgage on his house he only has three thousand of the fifty thousand that he won on a scratch card left, Dan decides to try his luck in a Casino just outside of town he is desperate for money, he walks in to the casino with three thousand pound cash and he feels lucky, Dan walks to the bar and orders himself a double shot of whiskey the Casino give him the drink "on the house" the bartender smiles, Dan then walks to the roulette tables, he spreads one thousand pounds worth of chips on the table and steps back watching carefully, eighteen comes out and he has fifty on it, he wins eighteen hundred pound he smiles but he knows it is not enough, he keeps the one thousand on the board and puts another thousand on it, he wins again this time with one hundred pound meaning he picks up three thousand six hundred pound, Dan feels lucky now "I am cleaning up tonight" he excitedly says to the dealer he has already nearly doubled his money he has five thousand six hundred on him, he feels like he cannot lose and in a crazy attempt to win big money Dan puts every penny he has on the board, he sits back, he appears to be calm but inside Dan is nervous and desperate to win, forty three, comes out Dan looks at the board only to see the number forty three looking back at him uncovered, he has just lost every penny that he had, in a daze he walks to his car and begins to drive, at first he is thinking about driving home trying to chase debts from his business but Dan knows that chasing debts can take months even years he changes his mind and drives to James Cohens's huge mansion.

Dan gets out of the car and starts knocking the door, a servant opens the door "can I help you?" the servant asks "I want to talk to James Cohens" Dan says "Mister Cohens is busy at the moment" the servant responds, I can book you an appointment to see him next week sometime, the servant adds as he holds out a notebook "go in to him now and tell him that Daniel Thomson wants to see him" Dan orders the servant, the servant slams the door as he goes to tell James that it is Daniel Thomson at the door, after five minutes he returns "come in" the servant politely says, "follow me" he adds, Dan looks around the huge mansion in amazement, there are antiques and valuable objects everywhere and the lobby is huge, Dan comes across a sign that says "the Cohens, the Chosen" the anagram and the ridiculous wealth of the Cohens family led's Dan to believe that James Cohens was chosen from the start. Dan follows the servant in to James's huge living room, there are two semi naked women with him, Dan asks James to make them leave the room, James looks at the women and points to the door they both quickly walk out of the room, James smiles "how can I help you? my friend" he asks, Dan is still watching the women the servant shuts the door leaving them alone "you owe me" Dan moans "I give you James, I give you all of this" he adds, James lights up a cigar "if you want my help all you have to do is ask" James calmly answers, Dan is surprised by James's answer "what is it you want?" James asks "women, drugs, fame or fortune, let me guess fortune" he adds "I need money, a lot of money" Dan says "how much" James asks "one million, two million, three fuck it let's say five million, will that do?" Dan nods "yes, that would do nicely, but when do I get it?" Dan asks, James looks at his calendar "you will have it in the next few weeks" he says, he pours Dan a drink, "you have my word" he answers Dan looks at the window he notice that James is very close to the castle and standing stones.

That night Dan gets back to his house, Justin and Clare are talking about a party at James's house Dan orders them not to go, Clare rolls her eyes and shouts "I am sick of you trying to control my life, I am eighteen, I will go to that party if I want to" she storms off upstairs, Dan looks at Justin "listen if she goes follow her and make sure nothing happens to her and keep in touch" Justin promises that Dan has nothing to worry about, he walks up to Clare's bedroom "are you going?" he asks "yeah of course, are you?" Clare asks, "Probably" he answers, and Justin gets ready to go out.

Its 9.00 pm before Clare and Justin get to the party Justin notices some very expensive cars in the car park and when they get in to the house they are surprised to see that the party goers are in most cases much older than Justin, Clare and James "well this looks fucking shit!" Justin whispers to Clare, an elderly woman over hears him, she gives him a filthy look and walks away, after a couple of minutes walking around the huge mansion Justin sees his friend Carl Cooper and a couple of Carl Coopers friends, Clare walks up to Justin and whispers "listen to how posh some of these are" she says, Justin listens to a conversation about ten yards away and just by listening to these people Justin can tell they are upper class, James is nowhere to be seen, after an hour and half Clare gets fed up and walks home, Justin text his dad to let him know that she should be back in about fifteen minutes, after ten minutes Dan looks out of the window and sees her walking towards the house, Clare walks in to the house straight upstairs in to her bedroom, Dan is just glad that she is home.

Meanwhile back at the party its five minutes to midnight, it’s a full moon Justin is talking to Carl Cooper, Carl is talking with two friends, they are talking about the recent murders that had taken place in this very house "lucky bastard" one of Carl's friends gasp as they look around the huge mansion "I would murder my parents for this house" the other jokes, Justin notices that a suited man is watching them very carefully, the clock strikes midnight and to Justin's, Carls and Carl's friends surprise people are ordered to leave the party, but they also notice a small amount of people are being asked to stay. Justin and his group are just about to leave when a servant stops Carl's friends "you have been invited to stay for the after party" the servant claims, Justin and Carl are ordered to leave, Carl is annoyed that his friends have been allowed to stay, Justin and Carl begin to walk home after five minutes walking they have to go in different directions, Carl shakes Justin's hand, he is just about to walk off, when Carl gets a feeling that he has left the keys to his house in his friend’s car "oh shit" Carl moans "what?" Justin asks, Carl explains about his keys being in William's car, "I have got to go back" Carl sighs, Justin agrees to walk back with him, when they turn around they notice a very dark and strange looking cloud, the cloud appears to be over James's huge mansion, "are we really going to walk towards that?" Justin asks "I have to or I am locked out all night" Carl answers, they both start walking back to James's huge mansion, as they are walking to the house Carl begins to hear something "do you hear that?" he asks Justin, Justin does not hear a thing at first but as he gets closer to the house he also begin to hear a deep sound, then as Justin and Carl get closer still Carl says "it sounds like chanting" Justin hears it clearly now and he remembers where he has heard it from before "I don't think we should knock the door" Justin cries but Carl is already knocking, there is no answer, Carl and Justin walk around the corner to where the car was parked, the chanting noise sounds close now, Carl walks up to William's car, "my keys are in his glove box" he moans, Carl looks up towards the standing stones which are at the Back of James's Garden, he notices people moving and Carl starts walking towards them, Justin shouts him back but Carl quickly walks off, Justin follows, he tries to call Carl back but Carl is quickly approaching the group of bodies, then Carl notices something is not right as he gets closer he sees that these men are wearing robes, they light a fire making it easier to see them Carl stops walking and he hides behind a huge tree and watches from a distance, Justin catches up and he also hides.

Justin and Carl continue watching as the fire that the group of hooded men have lit is burning well, some of the men are chanting when James walks out and stands on a rock placed just outside the castle, a crowd of about forty people stand, watch and listen to James as he begins to speak, Carl and Justin cannot make out what he is saying, Carl tries to move a bit closer for a better view, Justin follows, they hide behind a bush giving them a real good view but also making them easier to be seen, Carl is laughing "what the fuck are these freaks doing?" he asks, Justin is a bit more concerned "I don't know" he answers "but I really think that we should get out of here" Justin adds, two men walk from out of the castle, they both stand next to James, Carl notices that his friends are tied up, James starts another speech "everything that is good involves sacrifice we all make sacrifices everyday but today I make a special sacrifice, James lead's William to the centre of the standing stones, the crowd watch as James slashes the throat of William "what are they doing" Carl shouts, the whole crowd turns around looking at Carl and Justin, some of the hooded men have eyes that make them look possessed "fucking run" Justin shouts, they both quickly run through James garden back out on to the main road, when Carl sees a police car, he starts walking towards the car, the policemen pull over and get out of the car, they start walking towards Justin and Carl, as Carl approaches one of the policemen, the policeman launches a vicious attack on him leaving him rolling on the floor in pain, Justin sees a three foot but heavy branch on the floor and then he sees the policemen coming towards him, without thinking he picks the branch up and hits the young policeman in the face with it knocking him out, the other policeman tries to grab the branch but Justin moves away and bangs it of his head the policeman falls to the floor Justin tells a injured Carl to run they both run back to Justin's house.

Justin knocks the door there is no answer at first so he knocks louder, Carl looks behind them and sees the flashing lights of a police approaching, Justin bangs the door, Sally rushes to answer "it is one o clock in the morning, the children are asleep" she moans, she looks at Justin and notices he is out of breath "what's going on" she asks "wheres dad?" Justin replies, Sally pours herself a drink of water "Dan is asleep, so is everybody else in the house" she angrily answers, Justin tells Sally that Carl is going to have the spare room tonight "that's fine" Sally answers, she looks at Carl and says "the bed sheets are clean" Justin shows Carl to his room, Carl notices he has a view of the street, he starts to look out of the bedroom window when something catches his eye "turn the light off" he orders Justin, Justin turns the light off and walks to the window, he sees four police cars and three officers walking down the street "they are looking for us" Justin cries, Carl carries on watching he notices that one of the policemen is talking to a couple of robed men, "I am going to tell the police" Carl says as he heads to the door, Justin stops him from leaving "you don't fucking get it, do you?" he says "get what?" Carl asks "the police are protecting them, you go out there now and you will be arrested" Carl thinks about it, he thinks about the unnecessary attack the police officer launched at him, Justin walks out of the room its now 2.00 am and Justin is very tired, he is just about to go to bed when he walks past Clare's bedroom and hears her moaning in her sleep, as he enters the she sounds scared like she is having a nightmare and she looks restless, she is moving about a lot he walks out the room only to hear Dan also moaning, he opens the bedroom door and sees that both Dan and Sally seem very restless, Justin goes to bed.

Chapter 22. Aftermath

The next day comes and Justin gets up at 9.00 am, he walks in to the spare room where Carl slept, Carl is still sleeping, to Justin's surprise everybody in the house is still sleeping ten minutes later Carl wakes up he does not stay for breakfast as he needs to get home before his parents go out, Carl has dirty clothes on, a bruised eye, his ribs are hurting and he is walking with a limp, Meanwhile Sally comes down the stairs with Mandy, Mandy and Sally both look very tired "I had a bad dream last night" Mandy says to her mom, Sally thinks about it and answers "yes so did I, I can't really remember my dream but I know it was horrible" Sally adds. Carl steps out of the Thomson's drive only to see a police car, Carl tries to walk past without drawing any attention to himself, the policemen notice him and they start watching him walk past, this makes Carl feel very uncomfortable. Dan walks down the stairs like Mandy and Sally he is very tired "I was having some crazy dreams last night" he tells his wife "so was me and Mandy!" Sally answers, Dan is about to say something when the phone rings, he takes the call in to his office Sally shouts Jason downstairs and begins making him some breakfast when Dan walks back in Sally can tell that something is wrong "who was that?" she asks, "it was the police" Dan answers "at 7.00am they found my parents, dead" Dan starts crying "the police believe that a gang of thieves broke in to the house, woke them up and ending up killing them both to prevent themselves from getting caught" Dan explains, Dan is devastated. Carl is now out of the policemen's sight but it is not long before a different police car is following him Carl takes a short cut across a field to avoid them, he is glad to get home, he knocks the door and his dad answers "where have you been?" he asks "we were worried sick" he adds, Carl explains what happened and to his frustration and disbelief his parents dismiss his version of events "you think the local police force are protecting a group of devil worshippers? Grow up son" his father says, Carl walks up to his bedroom "I am having another couple of hours sleep" he shouts down the stairs, he lies on his bed and closes his eyes.

Dan has decided to drive to his parents house to visit the scene of the crime, after an hour's drive Dan pulls up at his parents' house, when Dan pulls up he sees two police officers looking around outside, as Dan enters the house is accompanied by one of them the other stays outside, Dan walks in to living room he notices that everything is tidy "what did they take?" Dan asks "nothing by the look of it" the police officer answers "we think that something may have distracted them" he adds, Dan walks up to the bedroom where the murders are said to have taken place, the carpet has blood stains all over it as do the walls Dan vomits and runs out of the room, "I have got to get out of here" he cries he starts rushing towards the front door when something catches his eye, he sees the same black stones that he brought from the Little Shop of Magik, Dan continues to vomit.

Meanwhile Carl is in bed but he cannot sleep, he gets up and walks down the stairs, he walks in to his kitchen he takes a knife out of the draw and is about to begin to make a sandwich for himself when he sees a small puddle of blood on the floor, the blood is coming from the small cloakroom, he puts the knife down and Carl opens the door and looks around, the cloakroom is fully of coats, jackets, boots and other things but Carl cannot see where the blood could be coming from, then he spots what at first appear to be two large black coats but on further inspection he sees that they are hooded robes, the same hooded robes he seen being used at the ritual, one of the robes is dripping with blood "what the fuck is going on" Carl gasps, he hears his parents car pull up, he quickly cleans up the blood shuts the door to the cloakroom and runs back upstairs in to his bedroom, he lays on his bed and he hears his parents walk in the house, suddenly Carl remembers he left the knife out, his dad shouts him Carl does not answer, he lays on his bed wondering what kind of people his parents really are.

After what seemed like a long drive back and the worst day of his life Dan gets back home, its only 7.00 pm but Dan is tired and goes to bed, "what is wrong with dad?" Clare asks Sally, Sally tells Justin, Clare and Jason to sit down "what's wrong?" Justin asks Sally explains what has happened to their Nan and Granddad, Jason begins to cry and so does Clare, "did they catch the people that done it?" Justin asks, Sally nods her head "not yet" she answers "don't mention it to Mandy, I will tell her when the time is right" Sally adds, she looks at Mandy as Mandy sits and watches the television.

Later that night it rains Justin and Clare are watching the rain through the window both are devastated about their grandparents, the rain is coming down fast, Mandy and Jason are watching cartoons on the television, Sally walks in to the living room and Mandy turns her head to look at her "are nanny and granddad with Mrs Morgan now?" she asks, Sally is shocked by what Mandy has just asked "yes" she answers, Mandy smiles "good, because Mr Morgan said they are safe with her" Mandy says, Sally is confused by the comment but she does not want to question Mandy at this traumatic time.

Justin and Clare see somebody walking down their drive "it's Carl" Justin says, Sally gets up and opens the door for him, Carl walks in the house he looks stressed and he is soaking wet "what's wrong with you?" Justin asks "I need to talk, alone" Carl says, Justin led's Carl to the kitchen and Carl explains how he is beginning to think that his parents had taken part in the ritual, Justin sits there listening but he does not react "hello" Carl shouts "can you hear me?" Justin looks up and says "yes, I can hear you" Justin answers "but we had some bad news earlier" he adds and he explains what has happened to his grandparents, Carl is speechless for a couple of seconds "sorry" he says, Justin is holding back his tears "what makes you think that your parents taken part in the ritual?" Justin asks, Carl tells Justin about the blood and the robes that he found, Justin is amazed "I am going to show you something" Justin says "follow me" he adds, Justin begins to walk down the cellar Carl follows.

Chapter 23. Antiqua autem edictum rufus.

On the way down Justin explains how he and his dad found a cellar by accident, Carl is quite interested, he explains about the statue, the coffins and the extra room they found, Carl is looking at the some of the old newspapers and photographs "there was a demon in the statue" Justin says, Carl laughs "a demon, you are joking?" Justin shows Carl some of the old newspaper articles on human sacrifice in Crudes Castle and demonic possession; although Carl is interested and listening he is not really buying the story "so what happened to this demon?" Carl asks, "he taken over James Cohens body and killed James Cohens parents" Justin answers, Carl begins to laugh until he looks at Justin, Justin is serious, Carl starts to look at some more of the old photographs "have you told anybody?" Carl asks, Justin laughs "yeah right, I would be sectioned" he answers, Carl notices a photograph he walks up to it a picks it up "that's my great, great granddad, I recognize him from old photographs my parents have shown me" he says pointing at Charles Cooper, on the same photograph Justin points at Henry Cohens "that is James's great, great granddad, he was also possessed by a demon, the same demon that now possesses James Cohens" Justin explains, Carl starts looking through more photographs and newspapers, many of the photographs have pictures of well dressed, well respected people on them, Carl Cooper points out that the photographs show "politicians, judges, policemen, business owners and even actors and musicians" Justin looks at the picture "I know" he answers, Carl looks at the statue "are you saying that a group of rich Satanists have somehow invoked this demon?" he asks, "no" Justin says, "this demon was here before them" he shows James newspaper articles that he got from the city archives "this newspaper article is from 1789, I printed it from the city archives" Carl reads about the ritualistic killings in Crudes Castle from 1789 and onwards "that's nothing" Justin adds, he shows Carl a huge list of missing people from the local area "why did the police not notice" Carl asks, Justin laughs "you really don't get it, they own the police!" he answers, Justin explains that James Cohens family were "superrich, aristocrats, high up masons with connections to the royal family, he is the owner of at least fifty different businesses, including the local shop and the Red Dragon pub" Justin uses his mobile phone to show Carl internet articles on the Ancient royal order of the red dragon. Carl is not believing any of what Justin is saying, Justin says "I can prove it to you" Justin asks Carl to give him a hand to move a huge cupboard that Dan blocked the passage way with, Justin shows Carls the huge tunnel "follow me" he says, Carl slowly follows.

After five minutes of walking Carl moans about the smell "it fuckin stinks" he says, "we are nearly there now" Justin replies, he walks in to the huge caved room, Carl is amazed a shocked when he first enters he looks around astonished by what Justin and Dan have found, Justin shines his torch around "look at the dead bodies" he says, Carl looks at the bodies "they look fresh" gasps Carl, Justin looks around "they are fresh" he says, he shows Carl a different entrance, the same one that Dan walked up "where does it go?" Carl asks "I don't know" Justin answers, they slowly begin walking down the tunnel after five minutes they see a light at the end of the tunnel "turn your torch off to save the battery" Justin tells Carl they walk out to the standing stones, Justin realises that the remains of the sacrifice victims are being hidden in the huge underground caved room attached to his cellar, they walk back to the cellar and Carl cannot believe what he has just seen. Carl looks at the time and says "I had better get home, I still don't have a key" Carl leaves and goes back home when Justin walks in to the living room Clare is still crying about the death of her grandparents, Justin walks out of the room he is about to walk up the stairs when he notices damp and bits of mould on the wall he assumes that the heavy rain must have caused it and he walks upstairs to bed.

The rain continues to fall and Carl is at home its midnight and his parents are now in bed sleeping, Carl creeps down the stairs and starts looking through the cloakroom, he notices that the robes have gone, he walks in to his father's study, he knows that his dad has never allowed him to go in his study so he is careful not to leave anything out of place, Carl's dad, George Cooper is a well respected judge, Carl slowly opens the top drawer on his dads desk, there is a small note book, Carl picks it up and looks through it, he finds nothing of interest in the note book or in any of the drawers, he is about to walk out of the room when a picture on the wall catches his eye, it's a picture of eight young men sitting behind a board, the board comes up to their waist and is about one foot wide, on the board Carl sees strange symbolism and Latin writing "Antiqua autem edictum rufus" he reads, he quickly takes his phone out of his pocket and takes a picture of the picture, Carl the creeps off back to bed.

The next day comes and the rain continues to fall, Dan has noticed that there is a leak in the roof "fucking hell" he moans as he puts a bucket on the floor to catch the water, he is looking at water slowly dripping from the ceiling when he gets a phone call from his parents solicitors, Dan takes the call in his office "my name is Adam Brown of Brown and sons soliciting services, first I would like to offer my deepest condolences for your loss, I have known your parents for a long time and they were good people. It is now my duty to inform you that your parents Clive Thomson and Margret Thomson left the sum of five million pound to you, they also left you the house" Dan remembers James saying "five million, would that be enough?" he puts the phone down and walks to his car "where you going?" Sally shouts but Dan does not answer. He gets in his car and drives to James Cohens huge house, when he pulls up at the house he notices that James appears to have a couple of guests, they are standing under a umbrella looking at the garden, Dan begins to walk up to James when a bodyguard stands in his way "Mr Cohens is busy showing these potential buyers around his house, come back later" the bodyguard says, Dan runs past the bodyguard, he is about to attack James when he notices James's face change, Dan can see the demon inside him, the husband and wife potential buyers also see it, James looks at them "what are you fuckin looking at?" he growls, the woman screams and holds on to her husband, James puts his hand in his pocket, he walks up to the woman and slits her throat her "no" her husband shouts in panic, James's face looks distorted and evil his eyes are dilated and he looks very angry, he punches the potential buyer in the face knocking him to the ground, he then jumps on top of him at punches his face repeatedly until his face is a bloody mess, Dan runs off, James's bodyguard watches in shock as James stands up "get a couple of the servants to get this mess up" James calmly orders his bodyguard, the bodyguard quickly walks off, James walks in to the house calmly singing, by now Dan is in his car on the way home.

Dan gets back to the house and Clare is in the living room, she is doing work on her laptop when Dan walks in to talk to her "Clare, promise me now that you will never see James Cohens again" he begs, Clare looks up "no" she says "he is not who you think he is" Dan explains Clare stands up "I am not discussing this with you" she cries and she storms off upstairs, the door knocks loudly, Sally is about to answer it when Dan stops her "wait" he says as he looks through the peep hole "its Carl" he says, Sally shouts Justin and Dan opens the door for Carl. Carl is eager to show Justin the picture that he found of his dad, Justin and Carl go upstairs and Carl shows him the picture "that's my dad" Carl says pointing at a man far left on the picture "Antiqua autem edictum rufus" Justin reads "what does that mean?" he adds "Ancient royal order of the red dragon" Carl answers, Justin looks at the picture, "I have seen this before" he says pointing at the strange symbolism and the Latin writing, he tells Carl to follow him and he heads down to the cellar, he starts looking through some of the old pictures that were left in his cellar, when he find a picture with a large group of men standing around the same board, with the same writing and symbolism on it, Justin looks at the back of the photograph, it has 1918 written on it, Carl and Justin carry on looking through some of the photographs. Meanwhile Dan is upstairs, he has now found a leak in Mandy's room he has also found damp and mould on some on the walls downstairs, he assumes it has been caused by the heavy rain that they have had recently.

Chapter 24. Storm.

After hours of searching through old photographs and newspapers that were left in Dan's cellar, Carl is reluctantly starting to become a believer, he looks at his watch and sees that it's getting late "I had better be going" he says, Justin shows Carl to the door, as Justin goes to open the door the wind blows the door wide open "are sure you want to walk home in this?" Justin asks, Carls nods his head "yeah I will be alright" he says as he walks out in to the rain and wind, Carl begins to run, Justin quickly shuts the door he walks in the living room and starts watching television with Clare and Dan, Sally is having a shower when the storm causes a power cut "I cannot believe this" Sally says as he searches round in the dark for her towel, Dan walks up with a candle, he puts it in the bedroom for her "what has happened?" Sally asks, "the storm has took the power out" Dan tells her, Jason and Mandy are sleeping and Dan checks that they are OK, when Dan gets down the stairs Justin and Clare are watching the storm through the window "the whole street has no power" Justin says, as he looks for the street lights "I hope Carl got back alright" he adds, Sally walks downstairs holding her candle "I don't like this storm" she moans as the rain falls heavier and the wind blows harder and the thunder and lightning begins.

Dan looks at his phone "it's nearly midnight, I am going to bed" he says as he walks out of the living room "goodnight" he shouts, Clare and Sally also go to bed, Justin looks out of the window, it's very dark and Justin cannot see much he is about to walk away from the window when he hears a huge crash, Dan comes running down the stairs "what was that?" he asks "I don't know" Justin answers "it seemed to be close though" he adds, Dan looks through the window but it is to dark for him to see anything "listen!" Justin gasps Dan listens, "it's somebody screaming" Justin says "it's probably the wind" Dan replies, then they hears another huge crashing noise, it sounds like thunder but it feels very close, Mandy wakes up crying and Sally quickly runs in to the bedroom to comfort her "I am scared" Mandy cries "why don't the lights work" she adds, Sally explains that there has been a power cut "can I sleep in your bed?" Mandy asks with tears coming from her eyes "yes" Sally answers, Mandy smiles "thank you mommy" she says happily.

The crashing and banging along with the thunder and lightning is keeping Clare awake, Justin and Dan are sitting downstairs, drinking a beer and watching the storm through the living room window, Justin looks at Dan, he can see that Dan is still hurting over the death of his parents, Justin wants to say something positive and supportive but he does not know what to say or how to say it, he is about to walk upstairs when Dan shouts "James Cohens killed your grandparents, you know?" Dan sips his beer and holds his tears back "there was no robbers, it was James Cohens" Dan adds, Justin is shocked "but why?" he asks, Dan begins to laugh at first Justin does not know what Dan is laughing at "what?" Justin asks, Dan carries on laughing he literally cannot stop laughing, he is hysterically laughing like a mad man, Justin looks very concerned "what are you laughing at, dad?" he asks, Dan stops laughing "We had no money, but we still had to pay the mortgage, we still have to pay for the car and other bills, so I asked James for help" Justin shakes his head and interrupts "you asked James for money?" Justin disappointedly asks, Dan looks at the floor "yes I asked him for money and he said that he would give me five million pounds, when my parents died they left me five million pounds after tax they also left me the house" Dan answers, Justin shakes his head again. Justin is annoyed and disappointed by his father's actions but he knows that his father probably did it for his family.

After an hour the wind starts to die down but the rains carries on falling and the whole village has no electric, at half past one Justin goes to bed, Dan stays up a has a more couple of drinks before going to bed drunk, he walks in his bedroom and looks at Mandy and Sally then a noise from outside gets his attention, Dan walks over to the window and looks, he sees an elderly woman standing in the rain, he believes it to be Mrs Morgan, Dan quickly runs to the front door but when he opens the door she has already gone "I'm am sorry I didn't listen" Dan shouts, he listens for a couple of seconds but hears no reply, Dan turns around and walks back in to the house, Dan is convinced that Mr Morgan was trying to warn him about the thing that was in his cellar.

The next day comes and the rain has finally come to a halt. Sally gets up first she looks at her watch, its 8.00 am Sally walks down the stairs and goes to turn on the television, the television does not turn on, Sally tries the light switch the light also does not turn on she walks in to the kitchen and looks in the fridge, she pours herself a glass of orange juice and goes to open the curtain. Upon opening the curtains Sally gazes in shock of what she sees "oh my god" she gasps she looks with disbelief at the damage that the storm has caused to the local area, there are uprooted trees lying on the floor and fence panels been destroyed and as she looks past her own drive she sees that roofs, chimneys and cars have been destroyed by the storm, Sally runs upstairs and wakes Dan, Justin hears her talking and he also looks out of the window.

Chapter 25. Disappearance

Justin is shocked he steps out of his house and walks up his drive, he sees that the houses are badly damaged and the whole area looks a mess there are police officers, ambulances and fire-fighters everywhere he looks, it looks like the end of the world to Justin, Justin goes back to his house he picks up his phone and he is about to phone Carl when he notices that the phones are down "shit" he moans, he opens the door and he is about to walk to Carl's house when Detective Mark Green stops him "hello, I am looking for a Mr Justin Thomson" Detective Mark Green requests "I am Justin Thomson!" Justin answers "come in" he adds, Detective Mark Green walks in to the house with his partner Constable George Jones "Do you know a Carl Cooper" Detective Mark Green asks "yes" Justin answers, Dan and Sally walk in to the living room "what's going on?" Sally gasps, Justin tells his mother to calm down, Detective Mark Green explains that Carl Cooper has been reported missing "when was the last time that you seen Carl Cooper?" Detective Mark Green asks, Justin tells the truth "he was here last night, he left at about ten minutes to midnight" Justin says "I told him to stay" he adds, Justin looks at Constable George Jones as he takes notes, Detective Mark Green asks a few more questions on the possible whereabouts of Carl Cooper and leaves the house, he leaves Justin and Sally his card "if you remember anything contact us immediately" Detective Mark Green asks before walking up the drive looking around for possible evidence "I hope your friend is alright" Sally says, Justin doubts that he is alright and Justin does not trust Carl's parents.

Its nearly half past ten by the time that Jason gets out of bed, he looks out of the window "no way, at least I don't have to go to school" he says excitedly as he looks around at the damage left by the storm he goes to turn the television on "powers out" Sally tells him "does this mean I cannot play the computer?" Jason asks his mom; Sally is annoyed by the silly question "of course you can't play the computer we don't have any electric" Sally answers "boring" Jason moans as he walks upstairs to his bedroom hoping to find something to do. Mandy is playing with her dolls in the living room, she is very worried by the storm, and Sally tries to comfort her.

Later that day Dan, Clare and Justin are looking through the old newspapers, photographs and other strange objects that they found in the cellar when Clare walks in to the room with the statue in it, Dan is looking at a photograph of Charles Cooper and the rest of the Antiqua autem edictum rufus or the Ancient royal order of the red dragon, "so do you believe that Carl's parents killed him?" Dan asks, Justin looks at the newspapers and photographs in front of him "I don't know but I do know that he had recently discovered that they are a part of this secret society" Justin answers, Dan is about to say something when they hear Clare screaming, they both go to run in to the room with the statue in when Clare comes storming out "what's wrong?" Dan asks "I really do not like that fuckin statue" Clare answers, Justin laughs "neither do I" he says, Clare turns her head a looks at the statue "but I dream that the statue is coming for me, I try to run but I can't I just panic and I hear it coming closer, I hide under my blanket at night and the footprints come closer and closer" Clare explains, Justin and Dan look at each other, Clare carries on "it comes in to my room and stands over me watching me sleep but I am not sleeping, I am pretending to sleep and hoping that it just goes away." Clare walks upstairs to the kitchen, Justin and Dan look at the statue; Sally is playing snakes and ladders with Jason and Mandy.

When Dan gets upstairs Sally tells him that they need more candles, Dan says he will drive to the shop "write a list" he says so Sally begins to write a list of thing that they need, when Dan gets in to his car he sees that there are a large group of council workers outside, Dan pulls his car over and begins a conversation with a group of them "do they know when we will have the electric back on?" Dan asks, "Not a clue" one of them shouts back "not tonight anyway" he adds, Dan looks at Justin he is about to drive off when a fellow council worker walks over to the group "this is so strange" he says "what is strange?" another council worker asks, this council worker has an identity badge on him with his name written on it, his name is Gordon "these trees appear to have been dying before this storm even started" the council worker tells Gordon, Dan and Justin listen to what is being said with huge interest, Gordon writes some notes, he looks at the trees and says "how do you know these trees were dying?" the council worker walks to the fallen trees "follow me" he orders, Gordon follows, James and Dan get out from the car and also follow "I have been a tree surgeon for twenty five years and I have never seen anything like this" Gordon looks around "what?" he says, "It is nearly June these trees should be beginning to bud but there is nothing" the council worker explains "in fact not one single tree in the whole of the village is beginning to bud, Justin and Dan look around, Justin remembers his hallucinations in these hallucinations Justin remembers that the trees were dead, "what could cause something like this?" Dan asks the tree surgeon, he looks around "some kind of poisoning of the soil maybe? But I really don't know as I have never seen anything like this before" Dan and Justin walk back to the car. Dan begins to drive to the shop "well that is strange" Dan says, Justin is deep in thought "it has got something to do with that statue" Justin says, Dan thinks about these old photographs with the lifeless looking trees "it's almost as if he feeds from the life of the village" Dan says. Dan and Justin arrive at the local shop, the shop is closed and the building has taken a hammering from the storm.

Justin and Dan decide to go on a ten mile journey to town "we have to have candles" Dan insists, Justin plugs his phone in the car charger as he cannot charge it at home, Dan is driving for about two miles before they notice the trees are a little greener, the further away they get from Crudes Castle the more green the trees seem to be, there are also flowers like daffodils "I have not seen a single flower growing in Crudes Castle" Dan says, Dan and Justin arrive in town, they are both surprised of how unaffected the town has been by the storms, they have rain and a few small floods but nothing like the level of damage they have seen at Crudes Castle. Dan goes to the shop and bulk buys tinned food and snacks "so we have to live on this shit?" Justin moans "I will get us a treat for tonight" Dan replies. Meanwhile Mandy is playing with her dolls when she hears a voice "Mandy" the woman's voice softly says, Mandy looks up "follow me" the voice requests Mandy gets up and starts walking to the front garden. When Mandy enters the garden she sees that Mrs Morgan looking back at her, Mrs Morgan smiles "thank you" she says to Mandy smiles back "I have to ask you to do something very important" Mrs Morgan explains, "Okay, I will try" Mandy says, Mrs Morgan looks at the floor "by your feet is a phone that belonged to Carl Cooper, give it to Justin and tell him to take a look through the phone" Sally is cleaning her bedroom when she notices Mandy is talking to a stranger, she quickly runs down the stairs and outside by the time she gets to Mandy, Mandy is alone "who were you talking to?" Sally asks, Mandy smiles and says "Mrs Morgan" Sally shakes her head "I have already told you that Mrs Morgan is dead" Sally sharply answers, she grabs Mandy by her arm and drags her in the house "you do not go out on your own again" she angrily says "I'm sorry mommy" Mandy answers.

Dan and Justin get back to the house with a load of candles, tinned food and other essentials, Dan has also bought take away food back with him, everybody rushes to the kitchen and help themselves to pizza and fries, Dan is eating his pizza when a black mark on the wall catches his eye "what is that?" he asks as he walks up to it "its damp or mould or something" Sally asks, Dan touches the wall and sees that it is wet "Bloody hell, more money that I need to spend" he moans. Justin is eating his pizza when Mandy walks up to him "I think that this belongs to Carl" Mandy says as she hands him Carl's mobile phone,

Justin is shocked "where did you get this from?" the police are looking for this Justin gasps "Mrs Morgan told me to give it to you" Mandy answers "she said there is something on there that you would want to see" Justin looks at the phone and sees that he has to enter a pin number to access the menu "well I can't look at it , I don't know the pin number" Justin says "five, seven, four, nine" Mandy says, Justin types the code in to Carl's phone and to his surprise the code was right "how did you know" Justin asks, "I just do" Mandy answers, Justin looks through the phone for ten minutes, he reads messages and looks at Carl's call records, there were no calls made after 7.00 pm "what am I looking for?" Justin asks "I don't know" Mandy answers, Justin walks upstairs with Carl's phone. After twenty minutes of look through his phone Justin clicks on to videos, he sees a video that was recorded at 1.00 am on the morning Carl went missing; Justin begins to watch the video.

At first the video is dark and unclear Justin cannot see or hear much apart from heavy breathing, then the camera points at two masked people they are wearing very dark demonic masks, very similar to Venetian masks, Carl screams "help, help" Justin watches intensely but the picture is very shaky "I'm sorry" Carl cries, Justin gets a good look at the mask, he also sees other people in the background, he believes he can also hear chanting, the chanting slowly gets louder and Carl stops screaming, "please stop" Carl begs "mom, dad please don't kill me" he adds the video comes to an abrupt end, Justin shouts his dad upstairs to watch the video, he explains that Mandy handed it to him when they were eating, Dan begins to watch "what are they doing?" Dan gasps as he watches; suddenly he has memories of his own experience "it's his parents!" Dan gasps as he watches "I knew it" Justin says. The battery on Carl's mobile phone is low so Dan and Justin take the phone to the car to charge the mobile phone, they sit in the car watching the video again, Dan alters the brightness and the contrast and pauses the footage "look" gasps Dan, Justin looks at the phone "that is James Cohens" Dan says "it is as well" gasps Justin "this is evidence we should hand it in to the police" Justin insists, Dan laughs "the police, we should sell it to the media" Justin is unsure but before he can argue Dan is already looking for media outlet contact details, he looks at Justin and laughs "we can make some money out of this shit" Dan insists after ten minutes he tells Justin "I have sent messages to five media outlets, I have told them that I have evidence that a young millionaire business and land owner is actually part of a murderess Satanic cult" he says "what now?" Justin asks "now we wait for a reply" Dan answers. Twenty minutes after sending emails to media outlets the police are at the front door "stay calm and stay down the cellar" Dan tells Justin as he slowly goes and opens the door "hello officers, can I help you?" Dan politely says, two police officers that Dan has never seen force their way into Dan's house "you can't do that" Dan cries, the two police officers look around the house "what are you doing?" Sally cries as the police officers search the upstairs, Mandy is screaming and Jason is also terrified.

When the police officers are looking around upstairs Dan quickly runs down the dark cellar he passes his phone to Justin and blows out the candles, the police officers walk down the stairs, they look around downstairs for ten minutes before one of them stand in the dark doorway of the cellar, the police officers look at Dan they grab their torches and begin walking down the cellar, the police officers see all the old newspapers and photographs, Justin hides under a desk watching them carefully, one of the officers walk in to the room with the huge stone statue, he walks around the room looking at many of the strange objects in the room then he shines his torch on the statue, he shines it right on the statues face, the statue appears to be looking at the police officer, he jumps back with a freight, suddenly his torch stops working so he tries to find a way out, he shouts his partner for help "Richie" he shouts, he hears nothing back and shouts him again but louder, he messes with the battery and his torch comes back on, he shines it around the room and then at the statue, to his amazement the statue still appears to be looking at him even though his is standing in a different part of the room, he quickly walks out of the room "Richie" he shouts "what" Richie calmly answers as he stands behind him "let's get out of here" the officer says "but what about the video evidence?" his partner answers, Justin looks up, Justin assumes they are talking about the evidence that Dan has sent to media outlets, this makes Justin suspect that the local police and the media are working to protect the young millionaire James Cohens. The police finally leave the house and Justin runs up the stairs "they were looking for Carl's phone" he cries, suddenly Sally walks in to the kitchen "why were the police searching the house?" she asks Dan smiles "I will explain later" he says, he then walks to the car with Justin.

Chapter 26. Arrested.

After a couple of hours Dan has still not had any replies from the emails that he has sent out, Justin and Dan are about to go back into the house when Dan notices police cars behind them, he looks around and sees that he is surrounded by four police cars, Detective Mark Green walks up to Justin and takes the phone "I do believe that this belongs to us" Justin and Dan are arrested, Sally storms out of the house "what are you arresting them for?" she shouts, Mark Green turns around and says "the murder's of Carl Cooper, John Jackson, Jack Gould and Anthony Collins" Sally is stunned, Justin and Dan are escorted to the police station for questioning. Sally walks back in to the house "come on" she shouts to Jason, Mandy and Clare, Dan watches them through the window has he is taken away in a separate car to Justin.

Justin and Dan are taken to the police station and put in to separate cells, Dan sits on the bed, he is obviously worried, he hears footsteps approaching Detective Mark Green walks in to Dan's cell, he takes Dan for questioning, Dan tells the truth about the phone "my youngest daughter Mandy found Carl's mobile phone, she handed it to Justin" he explains "ask Justin" he adds, Mark Green smiles we already have two police officers led Justin in to the room, Justin looks at Dan and he sees that Dan looks worried, he forces a smile and Justin sits down. Mark Green puts the phone on the table in front of them Justin and Dan look at the phone "there is a video showing the murder of Carl Cooper on the phone" Justin insists, Mark Green looks at his colleagues "where" he asks "in a file called my videos" Justin explains, Detective Mark Green begins looking through the phone for the video, after five minutes of looking for the video he hands the phone to Justin "where" Detective Mark Green asks Justin begins looking through the phone "it's gone" he cries as he searches through the "my videos" file. Justin starts searching other files "somebody has removed it" Justin angrily shouts. After they are both being questioned separately and then together Justin and Dan are led back to their cells, the cells are cold and dirty and Justin wants to go home, Dan appears to be lot more relaxed about the situation and he is quietly confident of being released in the morning. Meanwhile Sally, Clare, Jason and Mandy are at home with no electric Sally feels scared with so many murders and missing people in the area over the last few months she does not feel safe, they have candles lit and they are about to start eating sandwich's when the door knocks "who is it?" Clare asks as Sally peeps through the peephole "it's James Cohens" Sally answers Clare opens the door "come in" she politely says. James walks in to the house he is carrying two bags "where is your dad?" he asks, Clare explains that "he has been arrested" James hands Sally a bag of warm take away food and a bag of candles, batteries and other essentials “that is so nice of you” Sally says “thank you so much” she adds, James smiles.

They invite James to eat with them and James does not decline Clare shows him to the living room when Sally dishes out the food, James walks in to the candle lit living room, Jason is playing an old battery powered handheld computer “hello” James says, Jason looks up and then looks back down at his computer, Mandy is playing with her dolls she is very quite in the corner of the room and she has not even noticed James walk in yet “what have they arrested your father for?” James asks Clare, Jason looks at James and then back at his computer “I am not sure” Clare says as the truth would be embarrassing for her to admit “but it’s all a huge misunderstanding” Clare adds. Mandy stops playing with her dolls she feels something weird or horrible is about to happen she looks around the room and sees the most terrifying sight that she has ever seen, Mandy sees a ugly, demonic looking, non human entity in the living room with them, Mandy panics and screams, the screaming shocks Clare and Jason, Sally comes running in to the living “what’s wrong?” she asks as she runs over to her daughter “calm down” she whispers and Mandy slowly calms down, Mandy looks at James but Mandy does not see James the same way everybody else sees him Mandy sees the red eyed demon that is inside him, James looks at Mandy and she begins to scream again, she runs and hides behind the sofa. The incident embarrasses James “I am sorry about that” Sally says, Sally knows that Dan does not approve of James but Sally firmly believes that Dan has got James all wrong but as Sally watches Mandy and remembers some of the things that Dan has been saying about James Sally is starting to see that something is not right. Mandy peeps over from behind the sofa, after ten minutes James announces “I have to go now” Clare looks at him “where are going?” she asks “I have some business to take care of” James answers. He looks at Jason and says “bye, mate” Jason waves, he looks at Mandy and she looks at him before James even has time to say “goodbye” Mandy is screaming again, James steps back and shouts “I’m going, I’m going” but Mandy is still hysterically screaming, this makes James very angry, he walks out of the house and Clare follows and apologizes “I am sorry about my sister, are you alright?” she asks as James walks to his car “I’m fine” James replies, he starts his car up and drives on to the main road “why can she see me?” he shouts as he looks in to the mirror, he is so angry, his eyes turn black and he begins to shout “why can she fuckin see me” as he looks at his reflection, the more angry that James gets the more demonic his face seems to look he gets so angry that his face appears to morph.

It’s 3.00 am in the morning and Dan is sleeping in his cell, Justin is cold and he cannot get to sleep, he lies on his cold bed when he hears shouting, someone seems very annoyed then Justin recognizes the voice "its James Cohen" he whispers to himself, he hears his footsteps approaching Justin shuts his eyes and pretends to be sleeping when the door to his cell opens, the young policeman George Jones says "Justin Thomson, you are wanted in the interview room now" Justin is confused by this as is Dan when they tell him the news, they both sit in the interview room not knowing what or who they are waiting for when suddenly the door opens and to Dan and Justin's shock and horror James Cohens walks in to the room "hello" he calmly says, Dan looks at him James seems unstable and unpredictable "what do you want?" asks Dan, James smiles "I am here to get you out of here" he says "you are free to go" James says as he opens the door inviting them to leave, Dan stands up and walks to the door Justin follows him and they walk out. James is livid that he has to let them go and the young police officer George Jones looks terrified of James as he hands Dan and Justin back their possessions, it does not take Dan and Justin long to figure out that James Cohens wants them locked up and the police are working in his interest. Dan phones for a taxi as soon as he leaves the police station Justin looks back at James and the young police officer, James looks furious and he seems to be taking it out on the young police officer, Justin walks away quickly. Dan and Justin wait in a pub beer garden for their taxi to arrive "how long did they say they would be?" Justin asks Dan looks watch "about half an hour" Dan answers, Justin looks over to the police station and sees a car parking up outside the main entrance of the police station "its Detective Mark Green" Justin tells Dan, Dan looks over and sees the Detective as they are watching him walk into the police station their taxi pulls up "Daniel Thomson" the taxi driver asks "that's me" Dan replies and they get in to the taxi.

It's 4.15 am before they get back home, Dan opens the door, he flicks the light switch forgetting that the power was out, Justin gets in the house and goes straight to bed Dan lights a candle and pours himself a huge shot of whiskey and takes a few sips before topping it up, Dan is about to go to bed when he hears movement in the cellar, he grabs a torch and walks to the entrance and begins to walk down the stairs, he hears voices and the voices sound very familiar to him "who is there?" Dan shouts as he enters the main room of the cellar, Dan hears whispering "kill him, kill him" the whispering repeats Dan moves his torch around when he sees an elderly lady, it's Mr Morgan "you must kill him to protect your family and everyone in the village" Mr Morgan says, Dan runs off when he sees three other people this time it is John Jackson, Jack Gould and Anthony Collins "help us" they beg "kill him, kill him" they begin to chant, Mrs Morgan joins in, Dan hears a different voice, it is the electrician that allegeable committed suicide in the cellar “kill him, kill him” they all chant together, Dan sees his parents and James Cohens parents, Carl Cooper and then to his surprise he sees Constable George Jones they are all asking for Dan to kill James Cohens “free our spirits” his mom shouts. Dan turns around and sees James Cohens, this time he sees the real James, the real James that has been trapped in a dark empty world “help me” he desperately cries “please help me” Dan sees fear and pain in James and he feels guilty about what he has done “how?” asks Dan, James looks behind Dan, Dan turns around to see what he is looking at, there stands a very frail looking Mrs Morgan her bloodshot eyes look straight at Dan “you must kill him in a ritual held in your cellar” Dan shakes his head “no way” he says “no more murders, no more rituals” he insists, Mrs Morgan holds his arm tight “you have to kill him, bring him to the cellar” she screams, Dan wakes up he is surprised when he realises that he is in his bed and its 6.15 am lying next to Sally, he puts his arm around her and holds her tight, Dan notices something strange about Sally she feels different and she smells different, Dan looks at her as she turns her head to his horror and degust Mr Morgan is lying in his bed looking back at him “bring him to the cellar alive” she yells Dan wakes up again, this time its 9.37 am and this time Dan is not dreaming.

When Dan gets down stairs Sally is playing cards with Mandy and Jason she has spent the morning cleaning the house “how come they let you go?” Sally asks “lack of evidence” Dan answers “but they will be back, they are trying to set me up” he adds Sally looks at the floor “did you kill them” Sally asks, Dan pauses for a few seconds “no” Dan answers “James Cohens is trying to set me up” he says, Sally thinks about Mandy’s reaction to James, she tells Dan all about Mandy’s strange reaction “it’s as if she was seeing a different person to what I was seeing, she was terrified” Sally says “what was James Cohens doing in our house in the first place?” Dan asks “he bought us food and candles, I had to invite him in, it was raining” Sally answers “I don’t care if it’s raining acid I do not want that psycho anywhere near my house again” Dan angrily replies. Dan storms off to his office when the door knocks Sally opens the front door to see that its Detective Mark Green “hello again” Mark Green says calmly, Sally looks at him and she can see that there is something wrong “can I help you?” she asks “I am looking to talk to Daniel and Justin Thomson” Mark Green sternly tells Sally, Sally invites him to wait in the living room before going to Dan’s office and informing Dan “Detective Mark Green wants to talk to you, he is waiting in the living” Dan rolls his eyes and gets up off his chair “this is police harassment” Dan complains as he walks in to the living room “what do you want now?” he asks, Detective Mark Green gets to his feet “What time was you released last night?” Mark Green asks Dan thinks about it “it was about ten past three in the morning” he answers “what mood would you say Constable George Jones seemed to be in?”

Mark Green asks again Dan thinks about it "I don't know" Dan answers "I am not a mind reader" he sarcastically adds, Dan notices that Detective Mark Green looks upset "why do you ask?" Dan asks "this morning at three forty two I found his body, it appears that sometime between ten past three and twenty to four this morning Constable George Jones committed suicide by hanging himself in the staff bathroom" Detective Mark Green explains "was there anybody else with him when you left the station?" Mark Green asks "yes" Dan answers "James Cohens and he was pissed about the fact that you had to release me and my son" he adds, Mark Green walks towards the front door "that will be all thank you" he says as he opens the front door "wait" Dan shouts, Detective Mark green turns towards Dan "what happens now?" Dan asks, Mark Green looks at Dan and Sally "nothing, his death was a suicide, I have nothing on James Cohens other then the fact that he was the last person to see George alive and even if I did James Cohens has friends in high places he is literally untouchable" Mark Green answers, he shuts the door and walks to his car.

Justin is waiting at the top of the stairs he wants Detective Mark Green to leave before he walks down as soon as Detective Mark Green shuts the door Justin walks downstairs "what did he want?" Justin asks, Dan explains that Constable "George Jones had committed suicide in the early hours this morning, not long after we were released" Justin looks horrified and like Dan he suspects that James Cohens had something to do with his death "what did you tell him?" Justin asks "the truth" Dan answers "I think Detective Mark Green knows that James had something to do with it" Sally speculates "yeah but like he said James Cohens has friends in high places, he is untouchable" Dan adds.

Clare and Justin are talking in the living room "are you going to James's birthday party next week?" Clare asks "I did not even know that Justin was having a party next week" Justin answers "I have been invited, I had supposed to be there Friday night at ten o'clock" Clare says as she paints her nails "he has all of his business colleagues from seven until half nine" she adds "are you going?" Justin asks, Clare smiles "I am not allowed to go" she answers.

Chapter 27. Funeral

Today is the day of Dan's parents funeral and the Thomson family are on the way to the church, it's a small ceremony with not many people there just close friends and family, Dan has been so occupied that he has not really thought about the death of his parents, only today the day of the funeral it actually hits him. Dan looks nervous and he is drinking "be careful how many you have" Sally tells him as she watches him with a very concerned look on her face. The friends and family gather in the church for the cremation of Margret and Clive Thomson and the priest starts the ceremony, Dan sits next to Sally they are sitting in the middle of front row, Sally looks over at Justin, Clare, Jason and Mandy although Sally never really got along very well with Dan's parents she feels her children's grief and pain. Dan is sitting down, he looks calm and seems to be taking the whole thing very well Sally believes but suddenly she notices Dan look at the coffins, Dan believes he can hear something coming from one of them "did you hear that?" he whispers to Sally "no" Sally answers "what did you hear?" she whispers back "I don't know" Dan answers "but it seemed to be coming from the coffin" he adds, the priest stops reading for a second and looks at Sally and Dan "sorry" Sally whispers and the priest carries on with the ceremony. Dan is still listening out for the noise and Sally is watching him, Dan hears moaning "it is definitely coming from the coffin" he whispers to his "I don't think it is" Sally whispers back but Dan hears something else "it's my mom I recognize her voice" he whispers to Sally. Dan hears somebody at the back of the church he is laughing, Dan turns his head to see who could be laughing at his parents funeral when he sees James Cohens sitting on the back row with a huge grin on his face, Dan quickly stands up "what the fuck are you doing here" he shouts at James Cohens.

James Cohens does not flinch and the huge grin remains on his face, Dan starts walking to him ready to fight him when he is distracted by what appears to be his mother shouting for help "help me" he hears, he quickly glances at James Cohens and then turns towards the coffins, to his shock his mother sits up knocking the lid to the coffin off, she looks at him and says "save us Daniel, you must save us" the coffins begin to move towards the fire, with his mother and father appearing to still be alive "stop" Dan screams at the very top of his voice "please stop" he shouts again but the coffins are moving very close, Dan rushes to the huge fire and attempts to stop the coffins from burning but the heat from the fire is burning him too much for him to take, he backs off and watches as his parents scream for help as they are burning alive "help" Dan shouts, he turns around and looks around the church, he looks at where James Cohens was standing but Dan does not see James Cohens, he sees the demon that possesses James Cohen body, the demon is laughing as Dan's parents burn in front of him, Dan looks on the fire and screams he watches as his parents desperately try to escape from the fire, Dan desperately looks around for help but the crowd remain seated and calm as if they have not even noticed. Dan sees his parents melting as if they are in a furnace yet they are still alive, the demon smiles and says "their souls now belong to me" as he walks to Dan "and so does yours" he says as he pushes Dan in to the fire.

Dan wakes up in the church screaming and shouting Sally tries to calm him down but Dan seems hysterical and confused, it takes Dan a couple of minutes to calm down and realize that he was in fact dreaming. Dan slowly calms down and looks around the church, this time he sees that James Cohens is not at the funeral, Dan feels embarrassed as a crowd of people surround him, he is about to sit when he notices something on the chair that he had seen James Cohens sit on in his dream, it is a business card Dan quickly walks to the seat and picks up the card, the business card is James Cohens business card, Dan looks at the card and then looks around the church James Cohens is nowhere to be seen, Sally walks up to Dan and takes him back to his seat, Dan sits down and the priest continues with the ceremony. After the ceremony the family have a gathering at Margret and Clive Thomson's mansion, the mansion is now owned by Dan and due to the power outage at Crudes Castle Sally and Dan are considering spending a few weeks there "I will drive back to the house pick up some clothes and essentials for now, I should only be about a couple of hours" Dan tells Sally, "you have been drinking" Sally answers, Dan promises that is OK to drive, Sally is not sure about letting him go but she does not want to stay at Crudes Castle with no power tonight so she agrees, Dan explains to his guests that he has had an emergency come up and he invites them to help themselves to the drinks, Justin volunteers to give Dan a hand "thank you" Dan replies, Justin and Dan get in to his car and drive back to Crudes Castle, they do not intend on staying there very long "just pack some clothes and go" Dan tells Justin "after all we have everything we need at your grandparents house" he tells Justin.

Half an hour after Dan and Justin start out back to Crudes Castle most of the guests have already left Clare and Sally are cleaning up the house; Sally picks up the vacuum cleaner and takes it upstairs, Sally begins cleaning the upstairs bedrooms for the children, Sally thinks she hears movement coming from one of the bedrooms. Dan pulls up outside his house in Crudes Castle, he steps out of the car, Dan looks around, there are still no leaves on the trees and Dan gets the feeling the whole village is dying "what the fuck is happening" he says to himself as he pictures the house the way it was when the Thomson's first moved in. Dan walks in to the house and as soon as he enters the house he notices the place feels damp and cold and there is more mould on the walls then what Dan remembered in fact the walls are turning black and green in places with mould and rising damp, Dan just wants to get out of the house, it does not take Dan as long as he expected it to take him to pack the clothes and after only twenty minutes at the house they are ready to leave. Meanwhile Sally slowly walks in to the master bedroom, the bedroom is huge with strange art and ornaments everywhere then Sally notices a man sitting on the bed, she assumes that it is one of the guests but when he turns his head she is horrified to discover that it is James Cohens "James, what the hell are you doing here?" she asks James smiles and arrogantly answers "you."

Chapter 28. Betrayal.

Dan parks the car as close to the house as he can possible get it, he takes a couple of bags of clothes out of the car and walks to the house carrying them Justin also takes a couple of bags, when Dan gets to the house he is greeted by Clare "where is your mom?" Dan asks "she is upstairs cleaning" Clare answers Dan orders Clare to watch Mandy when Justin unloads the car and Dan walks upstairs looking for his wife, Dan hears movement and voices as he walks to the master bedroom, Dan feels that something is not right he slowly and quietly opens the door to the master bedroom and he slowly walks in, he is emotional crushed to see his wife is bed with another man, Dan watches for a couple of seconds before the anger builds up, he is about to explode when he notices that it is James Cohens in bed with his wife. James Cohens has seen Dan but Sally has not, James smiles "what's so funny" Sally asks as she continues to take the lead role James lays down "nothing, you're doing great" James answers. Dan storms out of the room but Sally is so busy that she does not even notice that Dan even seen them, Dan walks to his car a drives off very fast "where is dad going?" Clare asks Justin, Justin shrugs his shoulders.

Upstairs in the master bedroom Sally is laying in bed next to James already regretting what she has just done, Sally quickly stands up out of the bed and says "you have to go my husband will be back any minute" she walks in to the en suite and has a very quick shower by the time she gets out James Cohens has gone, Sally sits on the bed and thinks about what she has just done, she begins to cry when Clare walks in to the bedroom "what's wrong mom?" a very concerned Clare asks "nothing honey" Sally answers, she composes herself and begins to clean the bedroom "is your father back yet?" she asks "he has been back but he went back out in a hurry I don't know where he has gone now" Clare answers, Sally already feels a little bit worried. An hour later and there is still no sign of Dan, Sally is getting more and more concerned about his well being "did he tell you where he was going?" she asks Justin "no, he did not say a word" Justin answers.

Dan is in an off licence looking at the selection of alcoholic beverages, he picks up one litre bottle of whiskey and a one litre bottle of vodka before walking back to his car, Dan has decided to stay at Crudes Castle alone he has decided that he needs time to think. He walks in to the dark cold house and lights a candle, he walks in to the living room sits on the sofa and begins to cry "I cannot believe that she would fuckin do this to me" he cries, he pours himself a huge shot of whiskey and downs it, before refilling his glass, Dan is tired so it does not take him long to fall to sleep.

That night Sally is sitting downstairs at Dan's new house everyone else has gone to bed, the house is nice and comfortable but Sally feels low, she still not believe that she slept with James Cohens, she is thinking about how she let Dan and the family down, "but I could not fight him" she thinks to herself, Sally suspects that Dan might have seen them somehow, she picks up her mobile phone and calls his phone for the twenty first time tonight, Dan's phone goes straight to his answer machine, Sally turns off the lights and begins to walk upstairs.

The next morning comes and Dan wakes up in his bed when he first opens his eyes he believes that yesterday was just a dream until he looks around his bedroom and sees that he is alone. He walks down to the living room and pours himself a shot of whiskey, Dan then sits on the sofa, drinks his whiskey and immediately pours himself more, it is not even 10.00 am and Dan is drunk, he stands up and stumbles towards the front door, he walks to his car and starts it up, Dan knows that he is well over the drink driving limit but he wants cigarettes and alcohol so he drives regardless. First he drives to the local shop but due to the power outage and damage caused by the storm the shop is stlll closed, even though Dan is drunk he senses that something is not right with Crudes Castle, he looks around and the place looks dull there is no sign of life anywhere, the storm has left huge damage to many houses in the village, some of the houses have been left as they were as the families have been placed in hotels, trees uprooted from the storm have still not been cleaned up and even the local people look ill, tired and scared, Dan drives to town to get his drink and his cigarettes, he cannot get the image of Sally having sex with James Cohens out of his head. Meanwhile Sally is now very concerned about Dan "I am going to drive to Crudes Castle" she tells Clare "do you mind watching the children?" she asks, Clare agrees to watch Jason and Mandy and Sally begins the journey to Crudes Castle.

Sally is driving to Crudes Castle and when she arrives in to the village Sally also senses that something in the village is not right, the village looks dull and lifeless, Sally pulls up outside the mansion that the family had moved in to last year, Sally remembers the first time that she ever seen this place and how she and her family had such high hopes at that time, things feel very different now. Meanwhile Dan is driving back from town, he has a selection of alcoholic beverages, a box of two hundred cigarettes. When Dan enters his drive he sees that his wife's car is outside, Dan decides not to enter the property and carries on driving, he drives to the castle and the standing stones Dan parks his car and opens himself a bottle of vodka. Sally is in the house, the house is cold and damp and the mould seems to be getting worse by the day, Sally sees that mould and damp now cover the walls in the living room she slowly walks up the stairs in to the master bedroom "Daniel" she shouts as she enters the bedroom, the room is empty but Sally can tell that Dan has been there, she decides to wait downstairs hoping that he might return soon but after nearly an hour waiting Sally decides she has to go home she writes a note and places on the kitchen unit for Dan to read, she walks to her car and drives back home disappointed that she has not spoke to Dan. Dan is sitting in his car looking at the ancient castle and the standing stones when a huge cloud of mist suddenly covers everything, Dan steps out of his car he cannot see a thing but he can hear something, Dan quickly turns around to get in to his car but he his car is not where Dan thought it was, he turns around looking for his car but he sees nothing, he begins to walk through the mist after a few minutes the mist blows over and Dan can see again, he looks around for his car but his car has gone, Dan looks over at the castle and the standing stones, Dan is confused something looks and feels different, Dan begins to walk to the castle, the castle appears to be in almost perfect condition Dan looks around in amazement "what the fuck is going on?" he asks himself.

Chapter 29. Missing

He begins to walk towards the castle, Dan looks around confused by what he sees the whole place looks different, Dan walks around the castle and in to the ruins of the ancient village, only Dan does not see the ruins of an ancient village he sees a village that is still alive, he sees local people dressed in rags living in terrible conditions, there houses are small and many of them are made of wood "where am I?" Dan asks himself, one of the children approaches Dan "have you got any food?" he asks in a very strong Northern accent "no, sorry" Dan answers, the boy's mom shouts "don't be talkin to strangers" she tells him, she looks at Dan and pushes her child back in to the house, Dan feels a sudden drop in temperature he looks around and notices the local people are all rushing in to their homes, Dan senses fear in the people as they all go in to hiding "they are coming" a homeless man shouts as he runs in the opposite direction, Dan watches a mother rushing around trying to find her children, she seems in a huge panic when Dan sees something rushing towards the village, it seems to be a man in a black robe, Dan notices there is more than one, in fact they appear to be everywhere, within seconds the village has at least thirty men dressed in black robes and wearing strange masks walking through the village. Dan quickly hides in between two houses, he watches as a large group walk past him, then Dan sees a child standing his house "mom" the child shouts, the hooded men hear the child and quickly walk toward him, they grab him Dan rushes out but before Dan can do anything they vanish in to the distance. Dan runs towards his house as fast as he can, when he gets there he notices his house looks different, when the enters the house he notices that the tiles on the floor are different and the house has an echo, it feels cold, the whole house is completely different. Dan looks around for a few minutes before he hears footsteps walking towards him, Dan sees two hooded men he quickly hides behind a large wooden settle seat the men walk in to the room and sit on the seat.

Dan remains very still for five minutes until three more people walk in to the room "the rituals are about to begin" one of the hooded men says, they all walk out of the room except for one of them, Dan remains hidden, he peep's his head over and sees that the robed man is facing the opposite direction, Dan spots a brass candle holder, he picks it up and strikes the hooded man on the head, Dan takes his robes from him and hides the body at the back of the wooden settle seat, Dan looks around the house looking for the rest of them, then he sees one walking in to the cellar. When Dan gets down to the cellar he is shocked at how many people are there, the cellar has hundreds of candles and the crowd consists of about fifty men, all are wearing black robes and all have their hoods up, some of them are wearing masks too, Dan just observes for a few minutes amazed by what he sees. The hooded figures begin to chant one of the hooded men opens a curtain revealing the statue Dan looks at the statue as the crowd gasps "it is magnificent" one of the men in the crowd gasp, the chanting begins to get louder as a child is bought in to the cellar, Dan watches with horror as the boy is placed in the middle of the crowd, Dan sees the symbols and signs on the floor he knows that this child has been taken for a ritualistic sacrifice and Dan feels a strange energy in the room he looks around the cellar in order to find a way to stop the ritual, he notices an old axe in the corner of the cellar and slowly walks over to it and picks it up Dan slowly walks back to the circle hiding the axe in his robe, the high priest is loudly chanting Latin words and he is about to murder the scared child when Dan smashes the axe in to the head of the priest, Dan swing his axe lodging it in the back of a hooded man, he looks around there does not seem to be a way out for him, one of the hooded men walk up to him and removes his hood revealing a demonic and angry looking face, Dan wakes up on his sofa "what the fuck is going on?" he asks himself as he looks around his living room, he does not know how he ended up there.

Dan is confused he does not know when he is dreaming or when things are real anymore he stands up of the sofa, Dan can smell something bad he stands to the window and looks outside only to notice that his car is not there, Dan quickly runs outside looking for his car, he remembers parking it outside the standing stones so he decides to look there first, Dan quickly walks up to the ancient village ruins and the castle he is instantly reminded of his dream, when he gets to the back of the castle he can see his car behind the standing stones Dan runs to the car and sees the door is open, he looks around the car and much to his surprise the alcohol is still there. He jumps in the car gets the keys out of his pocket and drives home.

At Dan parents Mandy is watching television when a voice calls her "Mandy" the voice whispers Mandy looks up, only to see Mrs Morgan "follow me" the voice says Mandy follows Mrs Morgan. Sally is in the kitchen cooking "Do you want beans with your fish and chips?" she shouts, when there is no reply Sally walks in to the room and sees that Mandy is not there "Mandy" she shouts as she rushes upstairs, she walks in to Mandy's bedroom and sees that is also empty "Mandy" she screams, she opens Jason's bedroom door Jason is sitting in front of the computer like usual, Sally rushes to the bathroom she is not there so she checks her own room "Mandy, where are you?" she shouts she hears music playing in Clare's new room, she quickly opens the door to discover Clare in bed with James Cohens, she puts her hand over her mouth and walks out of the room "mom" Clare shouts as she pulls the covers over her "ever heard of knocking" she adds, Sally runs downstairs and phones the police “my child is missing” she cries down the phone.

Justin walks in to the house “have you seen Mandy?” Sally asks desperately “no” Justin answers, Sally explains that she “has gone missing and the police are on their way” Justin rushes outside looking around the house for her, he sees that she is not there “I will check the park” he shouts as he runs out the house, Clare walks in to the kitchen “I will deal with you later” Sally says, Clare rolls her eyes “deal with what?” she asks arrogantly Sally is about to scream at her “you jealous or something” Clare adds, Sally is silenced “he told me all about you” Clare reveals “I bet dad does not know or maybe he does and that is why he has left you” she adds, James Cohens enters the room “calm down ladies” he says “I can satisfy you both” he arrogantly boasts Sally looks at him with huge amounts of anger and she walks up to him with a serious look in her eyes, she grabs him pulls him towards her and starts passionately kissing him Clare watches she cannot believe what has just happened “fuck you mom” she shouts Sally backs off “I'm sorry” she says Clare runs upstairs Sally follows her shouting “I'm sorry” James calmly follows grinning on his way.

When Justin gets back to the house he sees that there are two policemen outside, Justin walks to the door “what are you doing” Justin asks “we are responding to a call made from this address by a Mrs Thomson claiming that she could not locate her seven year old daughter” the officer explains “we have been knocking for ten minutes but there is no answer” he adds “they must have gone looking for her” Justin explains as he opens the door “I will phone her and tell her that you are here” Justin adds, he phones his mothers mobile phone it rings on a kitchen unit “she has left her phone here” Justin says “what is the fucking point in having a fucking mobile phone if you're never going to take it fucking with you” Justin moans before hearing movement upstairs “Mandy” he shouts as he walks up the stairs, the policemen follow as Justin walks in to Mandy's bedroom but the room is empty, Justin hears movement from Sally's bedroom he and the police walk to the door, Justin quickly opens the door and he is instantly horrified, shocked and disgusted by what he sees. Sally, Clare and James are all in bed naked, James is smiling when Justin first looks at him, Sally refuses to stop having sex for a few seconds until Justin screams “mom, how could you fuckin do this” Sally looks at Justin and the policemen and then looks at James, James sarcastically smiles and waves as Sally realizes what she is doing “I am so sorry” she cries as she covers herself up, “where is Mandy?” Justin asks, Clare and Sally look at each other they feel embarrassment like never before “we don't know” Sally answers, Justin looks at her in disbelief “you mean your daughter and your little sister is missing and all you two can think about is fuckin cock, you fuckin whores" he screams before storming out "we need to ask some questions" the officer says "I will be down stairs in two minutes" Sally answers the policemen walk downstairs and wait in the living room.

Clare and Sally look at each other before noticing that James had disappeared, Sally quickly gets dressed and walks downstairs to answer questions, she walks in to the room living room and feels deep embarrassment she keeps thinking about how she acted earlier and she feels very ashamed "I am sorry about earlier" she says "I really do not know what come over me" she adds, the officer gets straight to the point "when did you last see your daughter?" he asks "guild me through what happened step by step." Meanwhile Justin is walking through the streets asking everyone he sees if they have seen a seven year old child, nobody seems to have seen her anywhere, he is so angry about his mother and sister but right now Justin's main concern is finding his little sister. Sally has been answering questions for twenty minutes now and the questions are starting to get more personal, Clare is sitting on the sofa with her head in her hands, the officers have called out a search party, one of the officers walk up to Sally "if your child was missing and you had reported it us why did you chose that time to go upstairs and start an orgy with whoever that was" Sally is annoyed by the question "that is personal, now get out my house and find my fuckin daughter" Sally cries "that is all" the officer says as he and his partner walk to the door "for now" he adds before leaving the house "we will be in touch" he says as Sally shuts the door, Sally and Clare look at each other, they feel embarrassed by what happened but confused to how and why it happened.

Chapter 30. Local hero.

Dan is eating when he gets a strange feeling that he is being watched, Dan quickly looks up and sees a little girl covered in mud, her dirty hair covers her face and Dan does not notice that it is Mandy until she looks up and says “daddy, I am hungry” Dan quickly runs to her “Mandy, what are you doing here, I mean how did you get here?” gasps Dan, Mandy collapses Dan catches her and puts her on the sofa, he walks in to the kitchen and pours her a glass of water “it’s all we got” he tells her has he passes her the glass “look at the state of you” Dan says as he holds her hand, Dan fills a bucket of water, he passes Mandy a sponge and shower gel “you will have to wash using this for now, we have no hot water” Dan tells her “I will be in my study” he adds, Dan rushes to his study and calls Justin, he tells Justin that Mandy is with him Justin is relieved “I will tell mom and I am coming to yours tonight” Justin says, he walks back to the house, he is getting more angry with his mother and sister by the second. Dan is about to leave the study when he sees a figure looking at him “your daughter is not safe” he figures cries, the figure steps from the darkness, its Mrs Morgan, Dan sees that she looks shaken and worried “he is coming for her” Mrs Morgan adds “who is coming” Dan asks, suddenly the door knocks and Mrs Morgan is gone, Dan looks through the peep and sees that James Cohens is at the door, he runs in to the living room, Dan notices that the smell is getting worse, he goes to hide Mandy behind the sofa when he moves the sofa forward he sees the corpse of the hooded man that he killed in his dream “what the fuck is going on” Dan gasps as he looks at the body he has no choice but to hide the body for now, he quickly hides Mandy in a cupboard at the back of the cellar “do not come out for anyone, wait for me to come back and get you out” Dan orders Mandy “O.K, daddy” Mandy replies, Dan rushes to open the door for James “what do you want?” Dan asks James walks in to the house and looks around “what are you doing?” Dan asks “just sit down and shut up” James orders “no fuck you” Dan shouts as he walk towards James, suddenly he falls to the floor, his body feels totally paralyzed “you should have done it the easy way” James says as he walks around the house, James moves the sofa but to Dan’s surprise the corpse had gone Dan feels as if he does not know what is real anymore.

James starts looking around the house after looking upstairs and most of downstairs he only has the cellar left and the study left, Dan watches as James walks to his study, Dan is desperate to escape when Sally walks in to the room “Sally, thank God” Dan gasps “you got to call the police” Dan desperately pleads “the police are already here, they understand what has happened here” Sally says “now where is Mandy?” Dan breathes a huge sigh of relief “In a cupboard at the back of the cellar, I told her not to move” Sally kisses Dan passionately, Dan begins to feel her breast "I want you now" Sally softly says as she takes of her top, Dan removes his trousers and Sally strips and leaps on Dan when they are interrupted by Justin "dad" Justin shouts as he opens the door to the living room, Justin looks at Dan in shock and disgust "what the fuck are you doing?" he cries to his dad, at first Dan thinks Justin is over reacting "we are adults" he says as he looks at Sally for support, only this time Dan does not see his naked wife he sees a naked James Cohens "shit" gasps Dan in a state of confusion "how the fuck could you do this?" Justin snarled at Dan is still confused he feels nauseated when he thinks about what he was doing seconds earlier "but I thought it was your mother" Justin laughs "yeah right, whatever" Justin mutters "he looks just like her but mom has a bigger dick" Justin adds "what the fuck did you just say?" Dan angrily shouts as he runs over to Justin, throwing a right hook and knocking to the ground, Justin quickly grabs the first thing that he comes across which is a fire poker, he hits Dan on the head with it as Dan tried to hit Justin again, Dan sees Justin standing over him ready to hit him again when Justin suddenly stops "where has James gone" Justin asks, Dan gets to his feet as fast as he can "fuck" he gasps as he remembers telling James where Mandy was, "shit, I told him where Mandy was" cries Dan, he quickly runs down to the back of the cellar Justin follows him, the cupboard doors are wide open and Dan knows she has gone "why did you tell him where she was?" Justin shouts at Dan, Dan has his head in his hands "I thought he was your mother" he answers, this time Justin believes his dad "it was your mother" Dan adds.

Justin thinks about what his dad has just said "maybe he tricked mom and Clare to" Justin accidently slips out "what do you mean he tricked mom and Clare" Dan angrily asks "shit" Justin says "I did not want to tell you like this" he adds, Dan is intensely staring at Justin "tell me what" he snarls "I caught mom and Clare together in bed with James" Justin mutters "what?" Dan shouts "I am going to kill that fuckin bitch" he adds, Dan punches the stone wall seriously injuring his hand when Justin grabs him by the shoulders "listen dad, I know what mom did was wrong but right now we have to concentrate on getting Mandy back from that psycho" Dan composes himself "your right" he says. Justin and Dan make their way to James Cohens house but when they get there the house is empty, Dan looks around when he sees a window at the back of the house has been left open "Justin" Dan shouts, Justin walks over "what?" he asks "go and have a look around inside, I will text you if I see anyone coming" Justin reluctantly climbs through the window. Justin sees there are security guards around the place, Justin sees that they are getting ready for James Cohens birthday party, Dan shouts Justin back "I have an idea" Dan says they drive back to the house.

They walk back to the house upon entering the house Dan quickly walks to his study and begins making a few phone calls, Justin is on his laptop reading the local news when James Cohens face appears on a news website, Justin follows the link and begins to read the story "Local hero donates five million to charities" the main headline reads, Justin reads the full article, the article portrays James Cohens as an hero and this angers Justin. Dan walks from the study and in to the living room he hands Justin a briefcase and says "I need you to pick something up for me" Justin opens the briefcase and sees that it is full of cash "I need you to take this to the Red Dragon car park and wait until you see a black BMW, when the black BMW arrives hand the man the briefcase and bring the package he gives you back home, do not let anyone see you" Justin agrees to go "he will be there and ready in about half an hour" Dan adds, Justin walks out the front door as he steps outside he sees Sally, Jason and Clare stepping from their car, they walk towards the house "where is Mandy?" I want her back" Sally insists Justin looks at her and screams "fuck you" in her face Sally watches as Justin walks away. She rushes in the house "Mandy, Mandy" she shouts as she runs upstairs in to Mandy's bedroom "she is not here!" Dan shouts Sally walks down the stairs "well where is she" Sally asks "your little fuckin toy boy has kidnapped her" Dan angrily answers, Sally storms out of the house "where are you going?" Dan shouts "I am going to get my daughter back" Sally answers, Clare follows her mother as Jason stays at thirteen Crudes Place with his father.

Meanwhile Justin is waiting at the car park when a black BMW pulls up Justin slowly approaches he hears the car unlock and he sits in the front seat and passes the man the briefcase, the man in the black BMW hands Justin a cardboard box, Justin takes the box and gets out of the car he begins to walk home.

Chapter 31. Preparations.

When Justin arrives home it is 11.30 pm "where the fuck have you been?" Dan asks "I had to take a detour, the police are everywhere" Justin answers he hands Dan the box and asks "what is it?" Dan opens the box Justin sees that the box is full of tablets, sachets and little glass bottles "what is it?" Justin asks again Dan laughs "enough hallucinogenic drugs to make James Cohens party, a party they will never forget, not matter how hard they try" he answers "but how are we going to give them the drugs?" Justin asks, Dan rubs his chin and thinks for a couple of seconds "you will see" he answers. Dan takes the drugs he grinds the tablets to a powder and bags them, he orders Justin to check on Jason which Justin does "he is fast asleep" Justin answers, "come on then" Dan says to Justin "we have to get Mandy back" he adds. He throws a mask at Justin, Justin remembers the mask from the rituals "what are you doing with this?" he asks "we are using them to cover our faces members of the Ancient royal order of the red dragon will be wearing the same robes" Dan answers "we are going to send that demon back to hell" he adds, Justin puts on the masks they begin to walk to James Cohens house unlike other houses in Crudes Castle James Cohens mansion has a generator solar panels and a wind turbine so James Cohens huge mansion still has electricity.

It is 2.00 am when Justin and Dan arrive at the mansion the tables are set out for the party, They look around hoping to find Mandy but they have no luck and with guards patrolling the house they decide they have to make a quick exit from the house or risk getting caught. Dan opens the fridge, he begins to put hallucinogenic drugs in the milk and the cream that are in the fridge he mixes them in the sugar, coffee, the flour and salt and the water dispensers, Dan sneaks in to James's bar and spikes all of the opened spirits with the drugs, Justin finds a shed outside with barrels of beer, he puts the hallucinogenic drugs in all of the barrels that are connected to the taps, when they are done they meet each in the kitchen "let's go" Justin says as he hears movement coming from upstairs, Justin and Dan make their escapes.

It is 4.30 am when they get home and Sally's car is still parked outside Dan opens the door and walks in to the house when he hears crying he walks in to the living room and sees Sally crying on the sofa "where is Clare?" Dan asks, Sally begins to cry louder "she has gone with that demon" Dan looks at Sally and notices a huge streak of grey hair "when did this happen?" he asks, Sally begins to cry hysterically "when I seen his true face" Sally answers, Dan and Justin know that she is talking about the demon that possesses the body of James Cohens "he is horrible" Sally cries "and he has my daughters" she adds James sends her to bed and tells Justin to "get some sleep, we have a big day tomorrow" Sally refuses to go to bed "we cannot leave them, we must call the police" she insists "we can't call the police, the police protect him" Dan answers "and I have a plan we will get her back" Dan adds after half an hour Sally falls on the bed a is asleep in minutes Dan stays awake thinking of a plan of how to get his daughters for an hour before falling asleep on the sofa.

The next day comes and the chefs at James's house are busy preparing the food, they are making soups, breads, roasting five different types of meat and making many deserts, Marcus is the head chef his three assistants are Tony, Richard and his best friend Greg, they are very busy today and Marcus is getting stressed "we have to perform today lads" he tells his team, he looks around and adds "this customer has some serious cash if we perform as good as I know we can and cook some kick ass food we could get more jobs like this" Tony and Greg roll their eyes "when is he going to pay" Tony asks, Marcus hands them seven hundred pound each "he has already paid" Marcus says Tony and Richard both smile and begin working, Marcus looks at Greg and laughs "I thought that would get them working" he jokes. Marcus is a short tempered chef but because Greg is his best friend and older than the other two he tends to show more respect to Greg than he does to Tony and Richard. Tony and Greg are chopping onions, tomatoes and other vegetables and Richard and Marcus are preparing the meats, Marcus walks towards a cupboard "we got no cinnamon" he moans, Tony quickly walks over and starts looking "just get on with your own job please, I am capable of looking through a cupboard" Marcus insists Tony gets back to chopping vegetables, Richard smirks at him "fuck you" Tony whispers. James Cohens walks in to the kitchen "Hello, Mr Cohens and thank you for choosing Diamond Catering, I do hope that we do not disappoint" Marcus nervously says as James Cohens walks through the kitchen, picks up an apple from his fruit bowl and walks back towards his front door "I am sure the food will be delightful, feel free to help yourself to the bar" James politely answers as he leaves the house "I will be back at about four O clock, we want the starters ready at about half past six" James request, he is escorted to his car by a security guard, Marcus hears Tony and Richard giggling "what are you two laughing at?" Marcus angrily asks "your tongue is so far up his arse" Richard giggles, Marcus slams the rolling pin on the kitchen unit "listen you little fuckin prick, you are getting paid a lot more than you are worth for this job so shut the fuck up and work!" Richard looks at the floor as Marcus is face to face with him "fuck this job up for me and I will fuck your life up" Marcus asserts "now I am going to get some cinnamon" Marcus calmly adds as he walks out the door, Richard goes back to cutting vegetables.

It is 11.00 am before Dan and Justin wake up, Dan begins to look around the house the mould and damp is getting worse and the walls are turning black, the trees look completely lifeless and the locals look run down and ill "what is going on with the house?" Dan asks "it is not the house it is the whole village and it is spreading" Justin answers, Dan and Justin both believe that the effects on the village of Crudes Castle are connected with James Cohens, the Ancient royal order of the red dragon secret society, the rituals and the statue in the cellar "Tonight he dies" Dan declares "how are you going to do that?" Justin asks, Dan smiles "tonight son we are going to a party, we are not drinking or eating anything from there but we are going to have a fucking good time, we are going to bring Mandy and Clare back home where they belong and we are going to send that fuckin demon back to hell where it belongs" Dan walks down to the cellar "I have a few final preparations to take care of" he tells Justin, Justin knows that he has no choice but to go along with his father's plan "what do we do now?" Justin shouts as his dad walks down the stairs "we wait!" Dan answers Justin walks in to the living room where he is confronted by his mother, she is crying "I am so sorry" she says as she hugs Justin "it is not your fault, that thing in James's body is not human" Justin tells her Sally cries again "what about Clare?" she blurts "we are going to get her back" Justin insists. Jason is outside with his friend, his friend is a few months older than Jason and he is known to be naughty, his name is Christopher Jackson "your house is haunted" he tells Jason "I know" Jason says, "the ghosts speak to me all the time" he adds "bullshit" Christopher replies "I will show you" Jason insists, Christopher looks at Jason "tonight, stay at my house " Jason says, Christopher laughs "if you are bullshitting I will break your face" he says as he walks off "meet you at the castle at eight O clock tonight" Christopher says as he walks away.

In James Cohens mansion his security are getting ready for the Birthday bash, as are the chef's, Richard walks over to the bar "do you want a drink lads?" he shouts over, Richard, Tony and Greg all have a pint of beer, Marcus stays on coffee for now. Tony goes outside to smoke a cigarette when the other three carry on with the preparations when Tony comes back in to the house he is on the phone "Tony" Marcus shouts, Tony puts his hands up "five minutes" he mimes, Marcus walks back in to the kitchen "Greg, go to the shop and get me some vanilla extract please" he asks, Greg puts his coat on and drives to town. It is Half past five and Tony has now been on the phone for over half an hour this angers Marcus because Marcus is stressed about time and unexpected visits to the shop have made time a valuable thing, Marcus walks in to the bar he can see that Tony has had a few drinks and this angers him "what the fuck are you doing drinking on the job?" Marcus rants Tony looks up and Marcus sees that he is crying "I am sorry" Marcus says as he walks out. Richard is cutting some carrots for the salad when Marcus walks in "I think Tony may have had some bad news" he tells Richard, Richard looks stressed and confused "what is wrong?" Marcus asks "my fingers, they are out of control!" Richard says as his hands are wriggling up and down his chest, Marcus sees James Cohens approaching the house "Mr Cohens is here so stop acting like retard" Marcus demands, Richard tries to compose himself. James walks in to the kitchen Richard is mixing a cake mixture "food should be ready right on time" Marcus says, Richard is staring at the mixture as he whisks, he goes in to a almost trance like state when he hears Marcus saying "Richard, Richard" very loudly as if he has been calling him for a while, Richard looks up at James and Marcus, at first glance Richard does not see James the same way as Marcus does instead he sees the demon that inhabits his body, he screams at the top of his voice and throws the whisk and the cake mixture at the demon, he attempts to run outside but he falls to the floor, cutting his head on the slate tile's in the kitchen. Richard stands up and looks at the demon in a panic, this time he sees the same as Marcus sees and that is James Cohens looking very angry and covered in cake mixture! Marcus grabs Richard to stop him throwing anything else "what the fuck is wrong with you" he screams, Richard is all apologies James Cohens is visibly fuming when he storms out of the room, Richard watches him as he hisses at him with a snake like tongue "did you see his tongue" Richard asks Marcus "just shut the fuck up and cook before I pick you up and literally throw you out of my sight" Marcus answers "now, where the fuck is Greg?" he mutters as he looks at his watch.

Chapter 32. Finishing Touches.

It is 5.30 pm and Dan is ready to go ahead with his plan, he is armed with a sword that he found in his cellar that he has placed in a sword holder under his robes, he passes Justin a sword "you might need this, but try to keep it hidden" Dan instructs Justin "what the fuck have you got planned" gasps Justin in a deeply concerned and fearful voice Dan laughs "tonight these fuckers will have a party they will never forget" Dan jokes "no matter how hard they try. Uppers, downers, MDNA, pills, medicinal drugs, LSD, Phencyclidine and many others on the menu." Justin and Dan begin to walk to James Cohens mansion they walk through the fields in order to stay out of sight. Sally has made Jason a sandwich as Jason sits in his room she takes it upstairs for him as she approaches the bedroom door she hears him talking, she opens the door "who are you talking to darling?" she asks "myself" Jason answers, Sally thinks he is lying and she looks around the bedroom.

Greg walks in to the kitchen "where the fuck have you been?" Marcus cries "did you get the vanilla extract?" he asks Greg passes him the vanilla extract "something very strange is happening to me" he says as he walks to the bar and pours himself another drink, Tony walks from the bar "oh so you have finished your phone conversation then, who was it?" asks Marcus "it was my mother" Tony says "telling me I am a disappointment and that I have let the family down", Marcus smiles "can't you talk to her when you get home and not when you are being paid to work?" Marcus asks, Tony laughs "not really, she has been dead for seven years" he adds Marcus snatches the phone a looks at the recent call list "you have not even had a phone call or text message since 9.15 this morning" he says as he looks through his call records Tony snatches the phone and looks for himself "what the fuck is happening?" he cries "I know it was her, she said I was an embarrassment to my family" he adds ad he sobs his heart out. There are many people arriving at James's house for the party and the house is starting to get busy "it's six o clock now" he mutters to himself "Tony chop some parsley for the soup" Marcus orders, Tony is still upset about his phone conversation he begins to chop the parsley, Marcus takes the freshly baked bread out of the oven and leaves it so cool down "get me a cola from the bar" Marcus orders Richard, Richard walks in to the bar and pours Marcus a cola. Richard is about to walk out of the bar when he hears somebody behind him, he turns his head and sees a woman covered in blood looking back at him, she looks angry Richard throws the cola's on the floor and runs to the door to escape "murderer" the woman screeches, Richard falls to the floor when Marcus walks in the room "what are doing?" Marcus asks as Richard is kneeling in a puddle of cola, Richard stands up and says "I feel ill" he runs outside and vomits. After cleaning himself up Richard walks back in to the kitchen "Just a few finishing touches before serving the soup" Marcus says as he sprinkles some pepper in to the soup, he serves six soups out and hands them to Tony to hand out, Tony takes the soups and walks in to the huge dining room "there are at least sixty people out there" Marcus tells Tony as he serves out more soups, suddenly Marcus is interrupted by a huge crashing sound followed by screaming, the crowd gasp as Tony runs back in to the kitchen "he is the fucking devil" Tony cries "are you fucking joking?" Marcus angrily snarls at Tony as he walks to the dining area "I am so sorry Mr Cohens" he says "I will get someone to clean it immediately" he insists James Cohens is annoyed but he is also concerned about why they seem to see through his disguise, Greg cleans up the mess as Marcus serves the soups and breads. Marcus serves the main courses as Greg dishes the food out and cleans the kitchen after serving the main courses and deserts Marcus walks in to the kitchen, Tony and Richard are waiting for a lift home and they both are feeling confused and suffering from mild hallucinations "there is something strange happening in this house" Tony cries, Marcus turns around and angrily stares at Tony and Richard "I know what is going on" Marcus says to Greg. Greg, Tony and Richard all look at Marcus waiting to hear what he has to say.

There are more and more people turning up to James's birthday party, the selected few that were invited for the meal with James Cohens are now finishing off with their coffees and getting ready to join the party, James's bar is getting busier and busier and as Dan had suspected many off the guests that are members of the Ancient royal order of the red dragon have come dressed in their robes, "they are ready for a ritual" Dan tells Justin as they approach the mansion dressed in their robes and harmed with swords. Dan and Justin are nearly at the entrance with Justin notices that there are security guards at the door "what if they ask for an invite or something" Justin asks "he didn't send out invites, I already checked" Dan answers, to Dan and Justin's surprise they are allowed in without even showing their faces, the guards even bow down to them as if they are royalty. Dan and Justin are in the party they are almost instantly asked if they would like any food or drink "no thank you" Dan says with a grin Justin also refuses a drink. It is eight o Clock and Jason is waiting by the castle for his friend Christopher, it is a full moon and Jason senses a strange atmosphere he sees his friend approaching and begins to walk towards him "what you got in your hand" Christopher asks "it's a book that I found in our cellar, this book shows you how to invoke spirits" Jason answers his friend snatches it from him "wow, this is well old" he says as he looks at the book Jason snatches it back "don't touch the book" he angrily tells Christopher "it's only a fuckin book" his friend replies.

Meanwhile Marcus is talking Tony and Richard "You to have been paid by Classy catering to infiltrate my business and fuck it up, haven't you?" he accuses "that is too far" he adds "what the fuck are you talking about?" Tony asks, Marcus feels paranoid and nervous "you can tell Mr Watson I will be speaking to my lawyer" Marcus insists, James Cohens walks in to the kitchen he does not look happy "I am so sorry about that" Marcus says, James Cohens walks past them not even acknowledging that Marcus spoke to him, Tony and Richard watch and see him shape shift in to a snake, Marcus angrily watches them as they watch James with their mouths wide open in shock "you two need some serious help" Marcus insists "now fucking clean up this place, I am going to the bar" he adds, Tony and Richard look and see they have a lot of cleaning to do. Greg walks up to the bar and gets a beer "one for the road" he jokes as Marcus has finishes his first "I will have a Shandy when I am waiting for those retards" Marcus insists. The party is getting very busy Dan has a huge grin on his face as he watches the party goers drinking their drug filled drinks and eating their drug filled food "what now?" Justin asks "now we wait" Dan laughs hysterically as he watches party goers showing the effects of the drugs, Justin watches him, he is seriously concerned that his dad is losing his mind.

Chapter 33. The Birthday party.

Jason and Christopher are in Jason's candle lit bedroom "do you want to see the cellar?" Jason asks "OK" Chris answers they take some candles and walk down to the cellar, Sally is sitting on the sofa rocking from side to side "what's wrong with your mom?" Chris asks Jason looks at her "she has been like that all day" Jason says Chris walks up to her and puts his hand in front of her face at first Sally does not react she seems to be in a trance like state but Christopher gets to comfortable and Sally suddenly stop rocking from side to side and looks at Chris, Sally sees devils and demons all around them she grabs Chris's arm tight "fuckin loose me bitch" Chris shouts in a panic "get out of this fuckin house now, get out of this village" Sally begs, Sally looks up at realizes she is not holding on to Chris she is actually holding on to a strange demonic looking creature with evil looking eyes! She punches, kicks and spits on it before noticing that it is Christopher she had launched her vicious attack on, he lays flat out on the floor with his face covered in blood "what the fuck have you done?" Jason screams at his mom she begins to rock from side to side again "Chris, Chris" Jason shouts as he shakes his friend in a desperate attempt to bring him back around.

Marcus walks into the dining room where only a few people remain he notices they look ill "I think we may of poisoned them" he whispers, Greg looks around and sees a happy crowd of about seven people, one of them wave at him, another one blows them a kiss, he looks at Marcus "they seem fine to me" Greg insists "are you joking?" Marcus asks "she just stuck her finger up at us and the other one puked everywhere" Marcus gasps as he rushes out of the room, Greg looks back he sees them looking and waving but he notices the floor is covered in vomit "what the fuck is going on" he cries. Marcus walks from the dining room to the bar he gets the feeling that everybody there is watching him "they are talking about us" he tells Greg. When Greg looks around he sees a party of dancer's and people having a good time "who is talking about us?" Greg asks "everybody here" Marcus answers "don't be stupid, you are being paranoid" Greg claims, Tony and Richard walk in to the bar "we are finished" Richard shouts at Marcus "good let's get out of here" Marcus says as he rushes to the door.

As the catering team are leaving James Cohens prepares to make a speech he stands behind a podium, Dan and Justin watch with interest as people around them are beginning to feel the effects of the drugs James taps his table to get the attention of his audience, everybody in the room turns to look at James four people in the crowd begin to hysterically scream claiming that they see the devil their screaming begin panic and hooded men (members of the Ancient royal order of the red dragon) restrain them using force this causes offence to a couple of their family members but they are also restrained "this is an historic day in Crudes Castles history, for today we will invoke the spirits of the Nephilim and ask the ancient ones for guidance as we advance our plan to walk among the living again and rule this planet again" The hooded figures cheer and applaud and the rest of the crowd follows with the cheering. James Cohens walks from the podium, cutting his speech short due to the chaos in the crowd he goes in to the back of his house, he walks in a bathroom "why can they see me" he snarls in the mirror. Meanwhile at 13 Crudes Place Sally is still rocking from side to side, Christopher is conscious and feeling better "what is wrong with your mom?" Christopher cries "she is probably on her period" Jason answers "drink some water it will make you feel better" he adds.

The catering team get in to their car, Marcus is driving he puts the key in to the ignition and turns it but nothing happens "oh no" he cries "please don't tell me I have to go back in there" he moans he tries to start the car again but again he fails the catering team begin walk back to the house. They step out of the car "I have a feeling something terrible is going to happen tonight" Marcus cries, Greg dances his way to the house, and Richard and Tony are just hoping to avoid James Cohens. Inside and the party is livening up Dan and Justin remain hidden under their robes, Dan looks around the party and it becomes obvious that the drugs he placed in their food and drink are beginning to take real affect, Dan looks at the dance floor and sees certain people dancing, their pupils I are dilated and their faces look twisted some people are lying on the floor struggling to walk and other are just staring in to space as if they have lost their minds, Dan also notices a huge increase in aggression as fights are breaking out all around him, he smiles to himself "now we have to find Mandy, I know she is here somewhere" Dan tells Justin, they both sneak off upstairs. Dan and Justin begin to look around the place but after searching three bedrooms upstairs they still have no idea where Mandy could be, it's a big house and there are over thirty bedrooms to search "we should separate" Dan suggests, they are about to go different ways when they are interrupted by footsteps approaching "hide in here" Dan says as he drags Justin in to a small storage room, they are hiding quietly when Justin notices cockroaches all over his legs "shit" he gasps as he starts moving around trying to remove them, Dan is also covered in them, in the commotion Justin knocks a box off the shelf making a huge noise the security guards walk up to the storage room and open the door, before the guard even get chance to ask any questions Dan pulls his ceremony sword out and cuts one of their heads off, he then pushes the sword through the other guards stomach before putting their corpses in to the storage room, Justin cannot believe what he has just witnessed, he vomits with disgust at the sight of the guards head.

Jason and Christopher are now walking down to the cellar Jason has the book in his hand, Sally is still rocking from side to side only now she is singing "My grandfather's clock was too large for the shelf, So it stood ninety years on the floor; It was taller by half than the old man himself, Though it weighed not a pennyweight more. It was bought on the morn of the day that he was born, and was always his treasure and pride; But it stopp'd short — never to go again — When the old man died. Ninety years without slumbering (tick, tock, tick, tock), His life's seconds numbering, (tick, tock, tick, tock)"

Marcus and the catering team walk back in to the party Marcus looks around and see's a lot of the crowd look ill, Greg is dancing his way to the bar and Richard and Tony are waiting by the exit, James Cohens walks through the party he looks around and sees nearly everybody there is acting strange some people are sitting in their own vomit and others are dancing, they are dancing as if they are in some kind of trance. James looks around and sees people fighting, he sees blood and chaos everywhere he looks as he turns his head he sees a woman lying on the floor, she is watching James and she looks terrified, the demon inside James knows that she sees the demon and not James, what's more is James notices that others are also beginning to see through his disguise "what is going on?" James shouts as he storms off.

Chapter 34. Light.

After hiding the bodies of the guards James and Dan separate and begin looking in different rooms, after looking in three rooms Dan hears a noise as he is about to enter the forth “who is it?” he asks as he walks in to the room, Justin is also about to enter a room when he sees a figure and he hears Carl Coopers voice “James Cohens is not the only demon here” Carl’s voice says “Carl, where are you?” Justin cries “look in the mirror” the voice says Justin looks and sees Carl in the mirror he is covered in blood and he has brutally scratched symbols on his body “I don’t have much time so listen good” Carl orders “spirits from all over the country are gathering around the village of Crudes Castle tonight, they are attempting to crossover in to your world to live again, some of these spirits are lost souls that have spent an endless amount of time trying to escape their empty world, others are truly cunning, intelligent and evil sometimes people do not even know the demon is inside them” Carl explains “it is up to you to stop them, they must be stopped at all costs but the more blood that is shed the easier it becomes for spirits to cross over to our world” Carl adds, he suddenly vanishes “how can I stop them?” Justin shouts at the top of his voice but Carl is gone, Justin looks in to the mirror one more time this time he sees one of the evil spirits, the demonic looking creature looks at Justin as rushes towards him Justin runs from the room in to the hallway.

James Cohens stands at the banister of the hallway above the crowd he looks concerned as the crowd below him seem out of control and some of them are seeing past the disguise that is James Cohens body, they are seeing straight in to his black soul. Dan watches and quietly follows as James walks down a long corridor in to his bedroom, Dan stands outside the room and hears that James is talking to somebody he peeps his head round and sees that James’s bedroom is huge and he has a woman in there with him. Dan hears Justin walking around, he quickly sneaks over to him “he is in that bedroom with a woman” Dan whispers “this is our chance” he adds. Dan walks to the storage closet and picks up a axe, he slowly walks up to the bedroom Jason follows, Jason has armed himself with a hammer, Dan rushes in to the bedroom swinging the axe like a mad man hitting James in the foot, he hears the woman screaming and instantly recognizes her voice “Clare” gasps Dan “dad, what the fuck are you doing?” Clare cries “you cannot stay with this man” Dan demands, Clare looks behind him and sees that James has got back to his feet, James picks up the axe and Clare raises a slight smile to him "you know what dad you are right" she answers as she watches James raise the axe over her father's head, James is about to swing when Justin hits him on the head with a hammer, the hammer embeds in to the skull of James Cohens he drops to the floor like a sack of potatoes, Justin and Dan look at Clare "she was going to let him do it" gasps a shocked Justin "you was going to let him kill your dad" he screams at her "I love him" Clare cries, Justin slaps her face Clare looks at Justin in amazement she cannot believe he has hit her leaving her with a bloody mouth. To Justin and Dan's surprise James gets back to his feet, this time his eyes are very dilated, James looks at Dan and hisses "are you going to show them?" he asks "show them what?" Justin asks, James looks at Dan and then back at Justin "show them.." before he could finish his sentence Dan smashes the axe in to his head, Justin looks at his dad. The spirit of James Cohens is wondering about in an empty, dark world when suddenly James Cohens see his corpse in his old house, James looks at Justin and Clare and smiles a light appears James Cohens begins to walk toward the light "we have to find Mandy" Justin cries, he looks around and sees Clare holding her face where he struck her but he does not see Dan "dad" he shouts there is no reply. Suddenly they are interrupted by screaming in the hallway "murder, murder" they hear, Justin runs in to the hallway and sees that a maid had discovered the bodies of two security guards "we have to find dad and Mandy" Justin declares, Justin and Clare hear the chanting begin "we have to be quick" Justin adds. Justin walks to the lobby and sees that the members of the Ancient royal order of the red dragon are preparing for the ritual, Justin assumes that the fact James Cohens is dead the ritual will be cancelled though the chanting continues and the hooded robed members of the Ancient royal order of the red dragon still prepare "they must have not found him yet" Justin whispers to Clare, Clare grins Justin sees security guards are looking around he tries to blend in the crowd.

The catering team are still at the party "how are we going to get home now?" Marcus asks Greg "I have no idea" Greg answers. Tony notices a woman on the dance floor he watches dancing for a few seconds, he recognizes this woman at first he is not sure where from but as he gets closer he is sure of who she is "mom" he gasps she turns around "Anthony" his mother softly says "but I thought you were dead" Tony mutters his mother smiles "no Tony, I just had to get away from you, you were nothing but a disappointment to me an embarrassment, that's what you are an embarrassment" his mother snarls in a spiteful tone, her eyes turn black and she scratches his face with her false nails, one of her nails are is lodged in his face Richard drags the woman off Tony "what is wrong with that bitch?" Richard asks, Tony with blood still dripping from his face grabs Richard by the throat "do not talk about my mom like that" Tony lets go of Richard's throat Richard is confused by Tony's actions. Suddenly the music from the party stop playing and the sound of modern day pop music is replaced by the chanting of the hooded men, one of the hooded figures begins a different chant as the others continue with the original chant. The hooded men stand in a circle and one of them begin reading aloud from a book. Justin looks around as the party goers gather around the hooded men the chants are getting louder and louder. Justin looks through the window he can feel the presence of the spirits, he can smell the sulphur like odour "the spirits are gathering they are ready to enter our world" the hooded priest shouts at the top of his voice. Justin is watching the ritual when he notices that Clare is gone he looks around for a few seconds when he sees seven children bought in to the circle, each child is holding a man's hand, though the men are covered in their robes, Justin sees that one of the children is Mandy.

Chapter 35. Gathering.

Jason and Christopher are still in the cellar Jason is ready to begin his attempt of communicating with some of the spirits of dead, Jason picks up the book and begins to read from it, a rumble of thunders leads them both to believe that there attempts are working, Jason carries on reading when suddenly a figure appears in the cellar "Jason" the figure says "granddad?" Jason replies, Jason approaches the figure "granddad?" he says again "I am not your granddad" the figure angrily scream as the figure's eyes turn red. Christopher watches Jason talking to himself "what are you doin?" Christopher asks "whatever it is, it's lame" he adds Jason turns his head towards his friend, Christopher sees his glowing red eyes and twisted angry looking face and runs out of the cellar and through the street. The streets are lit up by the full moon, the moon is red and looks the biggest he has ever seen it look Christopher senses a strange atmosphere Christopher is scared as he runs away from the Thomson's house. Christopher stops running he is exhausted so he sits on a bench not far away from the castle when he hears the chattering of a crowd Christopher looks behind him at first he sees orbs of light but these orbs change in to strange looking creatures, some of these creatures look confused and lost as they wonder around the village aimlessly but Christopher notices some of the creatures look evil and demonic in appearance. Christopher looks around him and he sees the orbs are coming from everywhere "what the fuck has Jason done?" he cries as he runs towards his house.

Justin watches as the children are lined up, the first child is bought towards the circle the hooded men carry on with the chanting as does the priest, the party goers are drugged up and most of them have no idea what is happening "I have to get the fuck out of this house" Tony tells the rest of the catering team he makes his way towards the exit Richard follows him, Greg looks at the hooded figures "this chanting is so cool!" he gasps Marcus looks up at Greg as he is still dancing "this music is fucking horrible" he argues "what the fuck is wrong with you?" Marcus asks Greg falls to the floor, Marcus quickly drags him to the kitchen "are you alright?" he asks as Greg opens his eyes a little Marcus gives him some salt water "what the fuck is happening" Greg asks "I just want to dance" he adds. Tony and Richard go outside Richard lights up a cigarette "this party is fucked" he exclaims, Richard notices Tony is looking at something Richard looks in the same direction "what the fuck is that?" he asks "I don't know but I cannot move" Tony says "neither can I" Richard replies, they feel a strange sensation as if they are flying, the next thing Tony and Richard know they are lying on the floor outside of the house, they quickly get to their feet and rush in to the house.

Justin is watching still hiding under his robe, he watches as the first child is bought towards the priest the chanting is getting louder and Justin notices that it seems to be having a hypnotic effect on many of the party goers. The child is placed in the middle of the circle and blind folded, his throat is slit, the crowd gasp in shock many of them begin to disapprove a jeer, Justin watches the boy's spirit walk in to the light but then Justin notices something else he notices two monstrous aggressive spirits fight for possession of his body, the priest stops the bleeding and begins a different chant, the priest is now in a trance after a struggle the weaker spirit backs off allowing the stronger and more aggressive spirit possession of the boy's body, the body of the boy stands up the party goers are amazed and absolutely stunned by what appears to be an amazing illusion the boys throat had even completely healed. Justin looks out of the window and sees that there are literally hundreds of spirits gathering around the house, orbs and strange figures are everywhere and people at the party seem completely unaware. The second child is handed to the priest Justin tries to walk towards the circle but he cannot get close enough as the circle of hooded robed men are stopping him, one of the men look at Justin and Justin looks back, the robed figure has the face of a demon, Justin is sure that the demons are claiming possession of the bodies and maybe even the souls of the secret society and the party goers he knows he has to stop this somehow. Justin looks around and sees spirits, lost souls and demons coming from everywhere they remind Justin of Vultures.

Justin is aware that the priest in going to kill the second child at the end of his prayer and the summoning of the spirits he knows he must act soon, the audience seem completely unaware of what is happening in fact most of them are staring in to space, dancing but they dance hyperactively and ridiculously they are chewing their faces off Justin notices that their faces look twisted and frightening, the priest continues with the chanting. Justin edges closer to the priest he holds his sword tightly the hooded men surrounding the priest are in a trance and still chanting as is the priest, Justin takes his sword out and decapitates one of the robed men, before anyone even reacts to what he has done Justin is rushing towards the priest reading to swing, he looks in to the priests eyes and he recognizes them he stops for a second and almost changes his mind when the priest picks up a ceremony sword and attempts to hit Justin, Justin rushes out of the way, Justin sees that the robed men are on to him and their faces look angry and demonic to Justin, Justin also sees the spirits of the dead waiting for a massacre he desperately swings his sword at the priest leaving a huge gash on his leg, the priest falls to the ground holding his leg in agony, Justin swings again killing a hooded man, Justin watches him drop after he buried the knife in to his chest but what Justin sees next horrifies him the most, he watches as a particularly evil spirit takes over possession of the hooded man's body, with blood still leaking from his chest the spirit uses the body he has possessed to kill more people in order to allow more spirits to cross through, Justin makes a desperate attempt to escape and he dodges three of the hooded men well running to the front door of the mansion. Chaos is everywhere and Marcus and Greg are still showing obvious effects of drugs they meet Tony and Richard "come on, we are going" Marcus tells them Tony and Richard do not react Marcus looks at them closely "why you acting like little girls?" he asks Richard and Tony remain silent, Marcus and Greg are about to rush out of the house when Richard launches an unexpected, unprovoked attack on Marcus and Tony does the same to Greg, Richard throws punches that knock Marcus to the ground, Marcus stops his carving knife sticking out of his bag, Richard approaches with a psychotic look in his eyes "please stop" Marcus begs, Richard dives on him throwing vicious punches and nearly knocking him unconscious, he is about to finish Marcus off when Marcus takes the knife and digs it hard in to his chest, he gets to his feet and looks at the corpse of his best friend and Tony standing over the corpse he sees red and stabs Tony in the throat "you fucking killed him" he screams as he watches Tony drop.

Justin is wondering around the house when he sees a telephone he rushes to the phone and picks it up, it has a dial tone unlike any other phone in Crudes Castle he dials 999 "emergency services, please state your emergency" the operator says "there has been multiple murders at the Cohens mansion at thirty six Crudes Castle" he cries "OK Mr Thomson, police officers will be with you soon" the operator answers "how did you know my name?" Justin asks the operator hangs up the phone Justin looks around and sees that he is being watched, a security guard walks up to Justin takes the phone out of his hands and head butts him in the face knocking Justin out.

Chapter 36. Awake.

The next thing Justin remembers is waking up in a hospital bed with both of his parents looking at him "what happened?" Justin asks confused by how he has ended up there, his dad looks at the floor "do you remember visiting Crudes Castle with your sister shortly after with moved there?" Dan asks "The night that I was drugged?" Justin asks "yes, that night" Dan answers "well they overdosed you on Lysergic acid diethylamide most people do not suffer from any further hallucinations within twenty four hours of taking the drug, you did! The doctors say it is a form of post traumatic stress disorder. You have been suffering from high anxiety, paranoia and even hallucinations" Dan adds, Justin is confused and stressed Sally walks out of the room covering her face and tears on the way out. Justin notices two police officers standing on the outside of his door "what are they doing here?" he asks his dad, Dan looks at the and shuts the door "the police believe that you are responsible for multiple murders that have taken place in Crudes Castle over the last twelve months, they want to ask you a few questions" Dan explains "you have to tell them about the secret society" Justin begs his dad, Dan looks confused "what about the secret society?" he asks "that's why we broke in to the party the Ancient royal order of the red dragon were planning a human sacrifice, James Cohens had kidnapped Mandy" he cries, Dan walks up to Justin and puts his arm around him "I am on your side and I will get you help" he insists, Dan walks out the door shutting it behind him "he is delusional!" he tells the police officers "I'm sorry" Detective Mark Green says as Dan walks away.

Justin is in hospital for days he notices that there are always police outside his room, he is feeling much better but still very confused Dan and Sally have bought Mandy, Jason and Clare to see him, Justin is very happy to see everybody especially Mandy, they bring him magazines and puzzles to keep him busy but after an hour they are being told visiting times are over. Justin is now walking about and ready to be released "when can I go home?" he asks, Sally and Dan look at each other "hopefully very soon" Dan answers before walking out the door. Justin lies on his bed reading a magazine when Detective Mark Green walks in to his room he is accompanied two other police officers "you're under arrest, you have the right to remain silent. Anything you say may be used against you in a court of law. You have the right to an attorney. If you cannot afford an attorney, one will be provided for you" Justin looks at the officers in horror he can see his parents are looking back at him his mother is crying as she walks away, Dan walks behind her Justin watches as his father limps off.

Justin is taken to the police station he waiting in a cell when Detective Mark Green and Constable Stewart Hall walk in to his cell, two police officers escort Justin to interrogation for questioning “for the record Justin Thomson has decided that he wishes not to have an attorney present” the Detective says loudly for the recording. Constable Stewart Hall take his seat he sits facing Dan, Detective Mark Green takes a folder of documents from a police officer standing at the door “that will be all for now, thank you” he says as he shuts the door, Mark Green sits down and looks at Justin in the eyes “do you have any idea why you are here?” he asks “no” Justin answers, Mark Green begins looking through the documents, he takes out a few photographs “do you know this man?” he is asked, Justin looks at the photograph “yeah its Dave the electrician he committed suicide in our house” Justin answers, Detective Mark Green takes a different photograph out and hands it to Justin “do you recognize these people?” Justin takes the picture “yes its John Jackson, Jack Gould and Anthony Collins” Justin answers, Detective Mark Green and Constable Stewart Hall look at each other, they hand him another photograph “how about these people?” they asks “that is Carl Cooper” they hand him a different photograph this time it shows James Cohens and his family Justin looks at the photograph when a flashback of him smashing James Cohens skull with a claw hammer comes back to him “do you know this man?” Mark Green asks “yes” Justin replies. They then show him pictures of the James Cohens how he was found by the police they show him pictures of James Cohens parents and his own grandparents as they were discovered by the police following their brutal murders “everyone that we have spoken about tonight is dead or missing” Mark Green sharply says “it seems that you are a very dangerous person to know” he adds “you cannot be trying to say that I killed all of these people” gasps Justin, Detective Mark Green smiles “John Jackson, Jack Gould and Anthony Collins drugged you, weeks later they all go missing!” Justin has flashbacks of the ritual in which they died, he remembers hiding their bodies “James Cohens, your mother and you’re sister are caught in bed together with police officers present, James Cohens ends up dead with a hole in his head, this was found next to his body and your fingerprints were on it” the police officers show him the hammer “the axe that was used has disappeared but what caught forensics attention the most were the strange symbols that were engraved in his skin, the same as your grandparents, same as James Cohens parents, Constable George Jones and the same as seven other murder victims from the night of James Cohens birthday party” Mark Green adds.

Chapter 37. Crazy.

Detective Mark Green and Constable Stewart Hall question Justin for a further forty five minutes accusing him of almost every unsolved murder and missing person that has taken place in the village of Crudes Castle since the Thomson moved in, they show him satanic websites that he has been "visiting regularly" and they claim they have more than a enough evidence to charge Justin Thomson of murder, Justin looks at all the evidence in front of him it is so convincing that Justin is questioning himself, he is taken back to his cell, when he gets in to the cell he sits on his bed thinking "maybe I did kill them" he thinks to himself "maybe I am crazy." Justin is falling to sleep when he has a sudden flashback of attacking the priest; he remembers swinging the sword damaging the priest's leg he remembers blood pouring from the wound. Justin then thinks of his dad "and I thought he was the one going crazy" he says to himself, he remembers his dad killing John Jackson, Jack Gould and Anthony Collins he remembers hiding the bodies with him. The more Justin begins to think about his father's actions the more convinced he becomes that his father is reasonable for at least some of the murders then he thinks about his dad limping away at the hospital "my dad was the priest" Justin thinks to himself. Justin begins banging the door a police officer approaches "I need to talk to Detective Mark Green" Justin insists "he is not here at the moment I will inform him that you want him as soon as I see him" the officer says, Justin still feels very weak and ill he rests while he is waiting for Detective Mark Green's return.

After just over an hour Detective Mark Green and Constable Stewart Hall return "I need to tell you something" Justin tells them, he is taken for further questioning and the conversation is again recorded by Detective Mark Green "what can we do for you?" Mark Green asks, Justin looks tired and weak "I think my dad may be the killer" Detective Mark Green and Constable Stewart Hall look at each other "the bodies are hidden in a secret passage going from the cellar" Justin concedes "there is a huge stone statue in the cellar too" Justin cries "it has something to do with that" he adds "is that all?" Detective Mark Green asks "I think so" Justin answers he is taken back to his cell "what will you do now?" Justin asks "we will search the premises to see if what you say is true if it is true we will take it from there" Detective Mark Green answers. Detective Mark Green and Constable Stewart Hall approach thirteen Crudes Place, they walk down to the cellar using torches to see where they are going.

After a few hours Detective Mark Green and Constable Stewart Hall return to Justin's cell and take him for further questioning, Detective Mark Green begin to record the conversation and Justin takes his seat eagerly waiting to hear what the police found in the cellar "did you look in the cellar at 13 Crudes Place" Justin asks, Detective Mark Green and Constable Stewart Hall look at each other "yes we did!" Mark Green answers "did you find the statue and the secret passage?" Justin asks excitedly "no" Mark Green answers "there was no secret passage and there was no statue" Constable Stewart Hall, Justin looks confused "shall I tell you what I believe Mr Thomson?" Justin looks up at Detective Mark Green "what do you believe?" Justin asks "I believe that you murdered John Jackson, Jack Gould and Anthony Collins as revenge for the prank that they played on you, I also believe that you murdered Carl Cooper, James Cohens, his parents and your own grandparents, why? I don't know maybe for money, maybe they were getting to close to the truth, maybe you have some serious mental health issues or maybe and probably all three!" Justin is stunned and he knows that Detective Mark Green's story sounds reasonable and realistic so realistic that Justin confused as he is, is beginning to believe it.

Eight months later and Justin has been spared prison after a judge ruled "the huge amounts of hallucinogenic drugs were found in blood and hair samples making a otherwise quiet, nice natured, young man paranoid and pushing him over the edge" Justin has been placed in a local psychiatric hospital, Justin thinks about his father limping out of the hospital and the court he then thinks of his attack on the priest on the at the ritual Justin is sure that is father was the priest but unfortunately for him nobody would believe if he were to tell anybody Justin decides he has to bide his time and get out of this place to do this Justin tells the doctors and nurses what they want to hear. Meanwhile Dan is at home his parents house he walks to his bedroom mirror and looks at his reflection as he looks he does not see the reflection of Daniel Thomson he sees the demon that has control of his soul.

To be continued?

www.ingramcontent.com/pod-product-compliance
Ingram Content Group UK Ltd.
Pitfield, Milton Keynes, MK11 3LW, UK
UKHW041935190726
13854UKWH00004B/1609

9 781304 909879